VOX DESPOTO, VOX POPULI.

THE IRON REPUBLIC

Richard Jameson Morgan

HEATHEN EDITIONS
THEIR BOOKS. OUR WAY.

Published in the good ole United States of America
by Heathen Editions, an imprint of
Heathen Creative
P.O. Box 588
Point Pleasant, WV 25550-0588

Heathen Editions are available at quantity discounts.
Bear witness to the yackety-yak and tomfoolery at:

heatheneditions.com

Social? Tag us! @heatheneditions
Photo? Tag it! #heathenedition

Caution: This book may alter your mind.

First serialized in *Florida Magazine* 1902
Heathen Edition published March 3, 2023

Paperback ISBN: 978-1-948316-45-3
Hardcover ISBN: 978-1-963228-45-8

Book and cover design by Sheridan Cleland
Set in 11pt Utopia Std
Titles in Molot

FIRST HEATHEN EDITION

CONTENTS

Heathenry: Thoughts on the Text vii

A Many-Sided Man xi

"Ah the Days." xv

"Them Sweet Old Days." xvi

The Iron Republic

    Chapter 1 1

    Chapter 2 9

    Chapter 3 19

    Chapter 4 25

    Chapter 5 37

    Chapter 6 43

    Chapter 7 61

    Chapter 8 77

    Chapter 9 95

    Chapter 10 113

    Chapter 11 131

    Chapter 12 139

    Chapter 13 147

HEATHENRY

Thoughts on the Text

We're in agreement with *The Tampa Tribune*: this is an "unusually interesting" story[1]—for several reasons.

First, its general setup is, in some ways, similar to Edgar Rice Burroughs' *The Land That Time Forgot*, which would arrive 16 years after this story, but whereas Burroughs ventures into Antarctic waters and discovers an uncharted island filled with dinosaurs, Richard Jameson Morgan ventures into—and through—Antarctic waters to discover an uncharted and bustling, highly-advanced utopian society.

The label "utopian," of course, being subjective as one man's utopia is another man's dystopia. A point Morgan cleverly examines via a religious zealot named Moses whom our main character J. E. Barrington encounters on a train near the end of the story.

Second, that brief interaction between Moses and Barrington addresses far more than the dichotomy of opposing utopian ideals as Moses wholly embodies the tangible dictum "seeing is believing." Religious fanatic though he is, he limits the Bible to "Divine Allegory" since his circumnavigation of the Iron Republic failed to produce an Africa, Asia, Italy, or Greece.

[1] Tampa Involved in a Thrilling Tale. (1902, February 2). *The Tampa Morning Tribune* 8(29). A9.

And since he could not look upon those countries himself, then the Bible's stories are, as per his logic, just that: stories—set in fictional lands. Anyone claiming otherwise is peddling "scholastic lies to deceive the credulous and make foundation for evil practices."[2] And that's food for thought because it presents you with the challenge: why do you believe what you believe? And how do you respond when someone counters your beliefs with theirs, especially when they have seen and experienced that which you have not? Inversely, how do you respond when someone denies that which you know to be truth? Do you respond the same way that Barrington responds to Moses?

Third, and lastly, the fact that this entire story came from the mind of an inventor-newspaperman-minister who only ever wrote one novella—this one—published as a serial in *Florida Magazine* from February through November 1902.

While most of the story is a lengthy discourse regarding the politics, economy, and government of The Iron Republic, enough sci-fi and forward-thinking is peppered throughout to make you double and triple check its original year of publication: 1902.

But one example being the paper napkins that *Kook Science* notes in their critique of the book: "The Iron Republic itself is what must be seen to be a communist utopia with . . . enough paper napkins for all." They're being jocular, of course, but the paper napkin disposal process that Morgan describes absolutely made us do a double take: "They were chemically cleansed and went into pulp again at the factory and so were used over and over."[3] Paper recycling. In 1902. Morgan was most certainly looking ahead. . . .

Now, as for the text, we took issue with Morgan's original six-chapter structure. Why? Because as we first assembled this edition, the original Chapter 3 was 36 pages, and Chapter 5 was a staggering 60 pages. Given that this is a novella, 60 pages

[2] p. 136
[3] p. 56

in a single chapter seems a bit tedious and unwieldy, especially considering the information conveyed in that chapter, and because nearly all of the other chapters were less than 10 pages each, so we have fractionated Chapters 3 and 5 utilizing natural narrative break points in order to make the text more manageable, resulting in a new chapter total of 13.

For transparency's sake, here is our breakdown:

Chapters 1 and 2 are the same as the original serial.

Chapter 3 has become Chapters 3 through 6.

Chapter 4 is the same, but is now Chapter 7.

Chapter 5 has become Chapters 8 through 12.

And what was originally titled "Conclusion," the sixth and final chapter, is now Chapter 13.

We've also corrected numerous instances throughout the story in which Morgan allowed two characters to speak dialogue within the same sentence or paragraph, which we always find maddening when you inevitably find yourself asking, "Wait: who's saying what?"

Further, we have collected and included three additional Morgan pieces that were published alongside the original serial in *Florida Magazine*. The first being a brief biographical sketch of Morgan titled "A Many-Sided Man" that provides the most information our research has been able to uncover about the can-do Floridian jack of all trades. The second and third being his poems "Ah the Days." and "Them Sweet Old Days."

(Forward-thinking in his fiction, but backward-looking in his poetry?)

All together, our edition includes everything contributed by, and concerning, Richard Jameson Morgan that was published in *Florida Magazine* in 1902.

With that, enjoy!

A MANY-SIDED MAN

Florida Magazine — September 1902

We have produced in this magazine the portraits of politicians, financiers, and men prominent in their professions and lines of work. We present in this issue a many-sided man and one who has achieved success in more different lines than perhaps any other citizen of the state.

Mr. Richard Jameson Morgan has become known to our readers as a polished and versatile writer, his latest contribution to these columns being *The Iron Republic* which is running in current issues. Mr. Morgan has the entrée[1] to the great periodicals of the country and is at present engaged in bringing out several books, the results of his labors for some years past. But, while he has achieved success in literature in the sense of doing good work and getting good pay for it, he seems to have found time for many other things as well. For years he has been a hardworking newspaper man and in this line has gained a reputation as one among the most incisive editorial writers, and by far the most original humorist in the south. He is also a popular lecturer on scientific, literary, and economic subjects, has appeared before the most cultured audiences north and south,

---

[1] In this context: the right to enter or join.

and is in demand as a star attraction at Chautauquas[2] and before learned bodies where his services are secured. He has many times been pressed by friends to devote himself entirely to the lecture platform, but says he cannot spare the time.

He is a diligent student, a classical scholar, and his work on antiquities and Biblical research have attracted attention. As an Egyptologist he is a recognized authority. He has also been a valuable contributor to the literature of the lost races of America, and his researches in that line have been extensive.

In addition to these things Mr. Morgan is a thorough mechanic and an inventor. His latest success in this line is the "New Century" printing press which he has perfected within the past year or two and which is now being manufactured by the Mugge-Morgan Co. at Tampa where they have a fine manufacturing establishment and turn out a complete printing press a day.

Mr. Morgan's inventions include printing presses, a telegraphic apparatus, a telegraphic writing apparatus, type-writer and matrix making machine, and an electrical express and mail delivery scheme, besides a number of mechanical movements and minor articles of utility.

So much for the subject of this sketch. The purpose of it is to point a moral as well as adorn a tale. This man whose life has been so full of labor and purpose was left an orphan at two years of age and has been on his own resources ever since he can remember. Without opportunities for an education in his youth, he has taken care of himself ever since he was large enough to carry a hoe to the cotton field, has educated himself, reared an accomplished family, and is yet but in the prime life and intellectual vigor. With it all he is a quiet modest citizen, content to take the lowest seat at feast or synagogue, and his

---

[2] Chautauqua is an adult education and social movement that spread throughout rural America and peaked in popularity in the late 19th and early 20th centuries, bringing entertainment and culture to communities, with speakers, teachers, musicians, showmen, preachers, and specialists of the day.

neighbors know him only as an unassuming worker and a burner of midnight oil.

Such an example ought to be an inspiration to young men everywhere and illustrates the possibilities of this great, free country to the poorest boy who tackles the problem of life seriously and with a determination to win.

AH THE DAYS.

Richard Jameson Morgan

Far o'er the meadow land
Bright golden bars
Upshooting, wide expand,
Out go the stars

Life's vast and might train
With new impulse,
Blindly presses on again,
With what results?

Hearts beat with passion strong
Ambitions high,
Then break. Ah, hapless throng
Surge madly by.

What hath the days in store
Above days past?
A sigh, a tear, a sorrow more,
Darkness at last!

Far o'er the meadow land
Pale amber bars,
Fade e'en as they expand.
Out come the stars.

THEM SWEET OLD DAYS.

Richard Jameson Morgan

Them sweet old days come back unbid,
    Inwove with good and ill;
And like ther old grey mule I rid
    Each Saterday ter mill,
Linger an' buck an' bulk behind
    Instid of trottin' out o' mind

I well remember how ther corn
    Wuz shelled ther night before,
An' in ther bright an' dewy morn
    I wuz started from the door
With "ride up Billy git thar soon
    An' try ter be back home by noon!"

But 'twa'nt no use. That summer day
    Slipt by jest like a dream,
And, as oft before, "I lost my way,"
    Or "raly it did seem
That folks from all the country round
    Hed got thar first to have thern ground!"

But one day, (ah, this thread of ill,
    Is wove in mem'ry's net;)
A squint eyed boy wuz at ther mill
    An' after we had met,

We hitched an'—then I seen blame soon
    Thet I could git back home by noon

An' ever after the fateful day
    I met that squint eyed kid,
I never seemed to lose my way
    No matter what I rid,
An' whether startin' late or soon,
    Wuz shore ter git back home by noon!

J. E. Barrington   **Captain Brent**

Captain Brent's ship *Wanderer* as she appeared on her return.
Photographed at Tampa.

With this number begins the remarkable narrative of Mr. J. E. Barrington, entitled *The Iron Republic*. It may be unnecessary for the Magazine to disclaim any responsibility for the truth of this extraordinary story. The writer claims to have absolute and demonstrable evidence of the truth of the article on board his vessel now lying in Tampa Bay, but we have not had the opportunity to inspect these proofs.

It is only fair to Mr. Barrington to say that he invites the public to come aboard his ship and see for themselves. Either as fact or fiction it is a rare story and presents an ideal of society and government that will make the average reader long to be a citizen of the newly discovered Iron Republic.

CHAPTER I

Dear Sir: Since the visit of your representative to my vessel, I have thought over the matter and decided to respond to your invitation to give an account of my strange adventures for the benefit of your readers. I write the narrative for your magazine because you have been kind enough to ask for it and because your interest and consideration is in marked contrast to that of other editors who have treated me with positive discourtesy, refusing to accept the statement of my experiences seriously. I am well aware that much of what I shall relate will appear incredible, and doubtless the whole story will be set down by many as a purely fanciful creation, like the fictions produced by Bellamy[1] and other theorists within the past few years.

About this matter, though I give myself no concern, as the many incontrovertible proofs, documentary and otherwise, which I have on board, will when presented to the proper authorities, receive the recognition of the government in due

---

[1] Edward Bellamy (1850-1898) was an American author, journalist, and political activist most famous for his 1888 utopian novel *Looking Backward: 2000-1887*. Bellamy's vision of a harmonious future world inspired the formation of numerous "Nationalist Clubs" dedicated to the propagation of his political ideas.

and proper form, as also that of geographical and scientific societies the world over.

I regret that my narrative proved, and demonstrated as it will be, must unsettle scientific theories and make it necessary to reconstruct some of our schoolbooks. But while this will result in temporary inconvenience and shake the faith of some in the dicta[2] of science, upon the whole the benefit will far exceed the injury. It is well to have our scientific theories unsettled every now and then, or we would become fossilized and arrogant like the bigots of the middle ages and oppose any further advance in knowledge.

It is unnecessary to say that after my narrative has been accepted, the Zetetic theory of the earth as a plane will have to be recognized and the geographies made in conformity therewith.[3]

In writing this history of my adventures, I wish it distinctly understood that I make no pretensions to literary style or ability and my account will probably be crude and faulty in many respects. My only effort will be to tell a round unvarnished tale true in every particular, for I realize that it is only in its truthfulness that the story can be of any value.

A man whose literary efforts have been limited to lawyer's briefs, few and far between, and whose supreme and most extended written effort was a spread eagle thesis on the science of politics, at the conclusion of an uneventful college career, cannot be expected to be a model of literary excellence.

But to come to my story.

In the autumn of '94, I was enjoying a comfortable practice in a flourishing county town in one of the great states of the

---

[2] Plural of dictum; formal, authoritative pronouncements.

[3] Based on conclusions derived from his 1838 Bedford Level experiment, Samuel Birley Rowbotham (1816-1884), writing under the pseudonym "Parallax," published the 1849 pamphlet titled *Zetetic Astronomy*, which he later expanded into the book *Earth Not a Globe* (1865), wherein he proposed the Earth is a flat plane centered at the North Pole and completely encircled along its outer edge by Antarctica. As Rowbotham explained: "The term 'zetetic' is derived from the Greek verb *zeteo*, which means to search or examine—to proceed only by inquiry."

Middle West. I say comfortable practice, because it was one that entailed very little work and gave me plenty of time to devote to society and politics, for the latter of which I had always felt a strong predilection. My father had achieved some distinction as an officer in the Civil War and afterward rose high in the politics of his state. It was the opinion of many that had he entered the arena of politics at an earlier period in life, he might have risen to the very highest office in the nation.

It has always been my desire to emulate his political career, and the prestige of his name with my strong inclination for public life, gave reasonable promise of success. Modesty forbids the mention of other reasons, though I already enjoyed some reputation as a speaker and was regarded by politicians throughout the state as a fighter and a "coming man."

I had adopted the profession of law as nearest allied to politics and a brass plate bearing the name of "J. Edward Barrington, Attorney and Counselor at Law," adorned my door, though I was known in political circles as Ned Barrington and a "live wire." There was no great demand for my professional services and I was not displeased that my social and political popularity far outshone my professional fame. The reader will understand my position when I say, by way of explanation, that I was not dependent upon my profession for support, my father, who died during my last year in college, having left an ample fortune for a young man of my steady habits and inexpensive tastes. And so, at the time my story opens I may say without offensive egotism that I was rather a promising young man of twenty-four, with a clear conscience, infinite digestion, and (I say it modestly) a fair share of good looks.

I was a member of the Young Men's Christian Association,[4] president of a flourishing literary club and had been for a year past the chairman of the Republican Executive Committee of

---

[4] Known today as the YMCA, it was founded on June 6, 1844, by English philanthropist and businessman George Williams (1821-1905), with an aim to put Christian values into practice by developing a healthy "body, mind, and spirit."

ch. ends p. 8

our county. I was also a leading spirit in a local Temperance Society[5] and was supposed to have considerable influence with the better elements of society in the town and county. I had never been a candidate for any office, but was a worker in my party, content to wait for my time. I am thus particular in these uninteresting details, because on them hinged the events that changed the whole course of my life, and gave me an experience that will, in all probability, make my name as familiar in future generations as that of Galileo[6] or Columbus.[7] The campaign of '94 was a particularly heated one. "Fatty" Burkheit, a notorious dive keeper, had been nominated by the Republican Party as the candidate for Congress from our district and a wave of indignation swept over the country. Meetings were held, several of which I addressed, and this action of the party was condemned on all sides. The district was Republican by a large majority, but many life-long Republicans declared that they would never vote for such a candidate.

The Democratic Convention had nominated "Buck" Magee, an expired fighter, of a reputation so unsavory that the alternative of voting for the opposition candidate was not to be thought of.

One evening in September, I was sitting before a comfortable fire in my library reading the evening paper, when my office boy announced a party of gentlemen. Supposing it was some members of the executive committee come to talk over the political situation, or a party of friends to enjoy a rubber[8]

---

[5] The American Temperance Society (ATS), also known as the American Society for the Promotion of Temperance, promoted abstention from drinking distilled alcohol or hard liquor, though beer and wine was permitted.

[6] Galileo di Vincenzo Bonaiuti de' Galilei (1564–1642) was an Italian astronomer, physicist and engineer and has been called the "father" of observational astronomy, modern physics, the scientific method, and modern science.

[7] Christopher Columbus (1451–1506) was an Italian explorer and navigator who completed four voyages across the Atlantic Ocean leading to the first known European contact with the Caribbean, Central America, and South America.

[8] In this context: a contest consisting of a series of successive matches.

of whist,[9] I had them ushered in. To abbreviate this part of my story as much as possible, it transpired that these gentlemen were members of the Democratic Committee and came with a proposition to cast the bulk of their party vote for me if I would permit myself to be brought forward as an independent candidate. They pointed out that the respectable element of the Republican Party demanded a candidate that it could vote for, and that with this vote and the support I would get from the Democratic Party, my election was assured. It is not necessary to dwell upon the details of that conference. Suffice it to say that the interest was so great and their reasoning so cogent[10] that I consented in the interest of morality and good government, to lead the movement. It seemed to be the providential opening to a great career, and when, in the enthusiasm occasioned by my acquiescence,[11] the four gentlemen (who seemed to be men of wealth,) shook hands with me and with each other and pledged a thousand dollars apiece in support of the campaign against corruption, I could do no less than hand them a check for a like amount.

This part of my narrative may be tiresome reading but it is a part of the story and in telling a story as in solving a problem, there is nothing like having all the factors stated at the beginning.

I will pass over the exciting events of that campaign; the speeches I made, the letters received, commending, warning, threatening even; the abuse heaped upon me by members of my own party, is all a part of the political history of the district. Up to the last week of the campaign, it seemed that my election was certain.

---

[9] A card game similar to bridge, and originally called whisk (from "whisking away" the cards after each hand), played by two pairs of players using a full deck in which the last card dealt indicates trump, tricks of four cards are played, and a point is scored for each trick over six won by each team.

[10] Clear, logical, and convincing.

[11] Reluctant acceptance or agreement without protest.

ch. ends p. 8

A few days before the election I was waited upon by a committee of "workers," with a letter of introduction from the chairman of the Democratic Committee, which stated that the support of these gentlemen was absolutely essential to my success at the polls. After reading the letter, I turned to the party, which had remained standing and asked what I could do for them. Taking the stub of a cigar from his mouth and squirting a lot of tobacco juice on my carpet, the leader a big-nosed Dutchman, made two or three awkward attempts to speak and finally blurted out something like the following: "dots all right cabding, you dond vanst ter ged lefd at der pallot box. Goot! Id dakes monish der make der mare drot. See? Ve vill gif you der subbort of der zaloon geepers for ten thousand tollars vich buts you in gongress vare you can makes id back on one vode. See? You puts oop der ten thousand ter shwing der vode ant goes to gongress; You dond put oop und sthays ter hoom. Und now vich is it?"[12]

And replacing the cigar stub in his mouth and putting his arms akimbo,[13] he looked for the world like a fiery fat jug with a handle on both sides. To say that I was astonished does not express it. I was utterly dumbfounded. The appearance of the men in my house had been an insult and when the vile proposition was made, it was more than I could endure and without standing on the quality of my English, I turned them summarily out of doors.

The balance is soon told. The Democrats voted solidly for their candidate as it was intended they should, and as I drew about fifty percent of the Republican vote, a Democrat was elected to Congress for the first time in the history of our district.

---

[12] Deciphered: "That's all right, captain, you don't want to get left at the ballot box. Good! It takes money to make the mare trot. See? We will give you the support of the saloon keepers for ten thousand dollars, which puts you in Congress where you can make it back on one vote. See? You put up the ten thousand to swing the vote and go to Congress; you don't put up and stay at home. And now which is it?"

[13] With hands on hips and elbows bent outward.

I learned afterward that if I had paid the ten thousand dollars it would in no wise[14] have affected the result. The money I did advance was not used in furthering my candidacy at all and the whole scheme was a device to divide and defeat the Republican Party in the district.

The morning after the election, I was the most universally hated man in the state. I was abused, ridiculed, cartooned. Life-long friends turned their backs upon me as a man who had sacrificed principle and sold himself in the vain hope of gratifying an inordinate political ambition. Some of those even, who had supported my candidacy, shook their heads dubiously and said there had been selling somewhere!

This, with the natural mortification I felt at having been used as a cat's paw[15] and defeated, thus cutting off prematurely my anticipated political career, made existence a burden and I determined to leave forever the scene of my disgrace.

But where could I go? My name was familiar from one end of the country to the other, even my features, from a half-page cartoon in a New York paper representing me as a cat's paw pulling out of the fire a most self-satisfied looking chestnut, which revealed the countenance of the successful Democratic candidate. After some bitter reflection, I decided to convert my property into money, and purchase a vessel large enough and strong enough to bear me beyond the confines of civilization, for only there did I feel that I could escape from the scorn of my fellowmen.

My eventful voyage, my discovery of the "Iron Republic" with its remarkable government and industrial conditions, my residence on this hitherto unknown continent, and study of its wonderful advancement in civilization and the arts of life, I will give an account of to the best of my ability in this narrative,

[14] "In no wise" is an archaic phrase meaning: not at all.
[15] An idiom derived from the fable "The Monkey and the Cat" by French fabulist Jean de La Fontaine (1621–1695), meaning a person who is exploited by another to carry out an unpleasant or dangerous task.

ch. ends next p.

which I trust may be as interesting as it is true. In the meantime the people of Jacksonville are welcome on board my vessel at all times, where they will be at liberty to inspect the many articles of interest which I brought from the land which lies beyond the ice barriers of the Antarctic Circle.

CHAPTER 2

As soon as possible after the disastrous termination of my first and last political campaign, I turned everything I had into gold and going down to New York bought the fine vessel which now lies in this harbor, somewhat the worse for wear, but still staunch and seaworthy. I shipped a good crew and a captain who had spent twenty years of his life playing hide and seek with icebergs as master of a whaler. My intention was to go on a three years' cruise into the Arctic regions and probably remain there, devoting the remainder of my life to the good of those isolated people, running the ship back and forth to the port of some civilized country.

After a conversation with Captain Brent, however, I changed my plans and decided to go south instead of north. My reason for this was that Captain Brent had done all of his whaling in southern waters and was familiar with every piece of terra firma[1] from the straits of Magellan[2] to Kirguelan's Land[3] and knew nothing whatever about the Arctic regions. And inasmuch

---

[1] Dry land.

[2] The Strait of Magellan, considered the most important natural passage between the Atlantic and Pacific oceans, is a navigable sea route in southern Chile separating mainland South America to the north and Tierra del Fuego to the south.

[3] The Kerguelen Islands, also known as the Desolation Islands because they are among the most isolated places on Earth, are a group of islands in the sub-Antarctic.

as my object was to get away and as far away as possible from the haunts of civilized men, I readily agreed and drew the papers for a three years' cruise to extend as far south as I should desire, "open water permitting."

On the 17th day of June 1895, having on board stores for a three years' cruise, fifty thousand dollars in gold coin in an iron safe[4] in my private cabin and a picked crew. I sailed out of New York harbor literally shaking the dust of my native country from my feet, and carrying a lighter heart than I had for months past.

It is not necessary to draw out and magnify the incidents of this voyage. There are writers, (W. Clark Russel[5] for instance,) whose business in life is to describe sea voyages. The chief interest in this story must lie in what was accomplished by the voyage and not the voyage itself. In my cabin with my books, under an awning on the poop[6] with Captain Brent—who was extremely well informed for a seaman—or making myself at home with the sailors before the mast, every hour was pleasantly employed. Winds were very favorable considering the season of the year and we drew down rapidly toward the tropics.

On the 10th of August we crossed the equator and I brought out half dozen bottles of wine and a box of cigars and had the sailors, who were all smart American boys, aft.[7] About the last of September, we passed the cape and began to realize that we were indeed leaving the habitable world and passing into a solitude of waters whose southern boundaries were unknown. And here our real voyage began.

There is a fierceness and blackness in these wild waters below the cape that those familiar only with the ship courses of the Atlantic and Pacific can form no conception of. Wilder and wilder grew the sea as we drew southward, but Captain

---

[4] Adjusted for inflation (1895-2023), that was approximately $1.7M.

[5] William Clark Russell (1844-1911) was an English writer best known for his nautical novels.

[6] Poop deck; the highest deck of a ship, generally in the stern (rear) and forming the roof of a cabin.

[7] At, near, or toward the stern (the rearmost part) of a ship or boat.

Brent was an old navigator and I feared the terrors of the whole Antarctic region not so much as a single cartoon in an American newspaper.

In a hundred and fifty-one days after leaving New York, we encountered ice and a month later, we were sailing along the southern ice barriers that towered like sapphire cliffs as far as the eye could see in either direction. It was now summer time in these regions and Captain Brent said he had never seen the sea so clear of ice. Whales spouted in every direction and sea fowl by thousands sailed above us or perched among the icy precipices. The grandeur of the scenery about us at this time baffles description. As we sailed leisurely east by south, there was a wall of ice on our right, ranging from fifty to three hundred feet high, giving out with a splendor which no artist may portray, the gorgeous hues of the rainbow. In some places, the cliffs overhung making great grottoes[8] in which the largest ship might float.

On the 23rd of December we sighted the lofty summit of Mount Erebus, the only volcano, so far as is known in the Antarctic regions.[9] On the 29th, turning a spur or promontory of ice that jutted out many miles into the sea, we ran into a great cove land-locked, or rather ice-locked, where the water was smooth and where the cliffs shelved up gradually from the water's edge, reaching back and up many thousand feet, to where the opal tinted ice shaded off into the dull gray and brown of the rugged and barren rocks of Mount Erebus.

Standing on the deck of the ship and looking up the wide and irregular incline of ice that extended from the water's edge up to where the rugged sides of Mount Erebus showed above, I enjoyed one of the grandest sights ever looked upon by man. This sloping incline was broken into hundreds of terraces down which the melting snow water dashed in innumerable cascades

[8] Small caves or caverns.
[9] Mount Erebus on Ross Island, Antarctica, is the second-highest volcano in Antarctica (after Mount Sidley), and the southernmost active volcano on Earth.

ch. ends p. 17

and poured into the sea, making great banks of fleecy foam that froze and floated away, as it were, gossamer icebergs.

As I gazed up this terraced incline from the placid sea to the towering heights beyond, it looked like a marble stairway leading up to heaven, so broad and grand in its mighty sweep that all the tribes of earth might mount upon it. It was a picture that Milton[10] or Homer[11] might have used in their immortal epics of gods and angels.

The water lapping over terraces and leaping downward here and there was as white as milk and in the distance looked like gauzy draperies of lace and down spread on the mighty stairway, as archangels might spread them for gods to walk upon. No grander sight was ever looked upon by seer or prophet in the most enraptured vision.

This phenomenon, so remarkable in these regions of ice and snow, where the temperature is always below the freezing point, was caused by the heat of Mount Erebus melting the ice and snow that climbed up its sides for thousands of feet. The volcano was in a mild state of eruption and I suppose the hidden fires on this side had melted down the ice walls and worn away this great thoroughfare to the sea by pouring down a continuous flood of water. The ascent looked accessible and I determined to make an effort to reach the great cone and have a view of these unknown regions. We had Christmas dinner on board, after which Captain Brent read from his manual a service suitable for the occasion, and perhaps with the exception of myself, everyone on the ship yearned for home and its associations on this day of universal joy and gladness. The boys looked blue enough until I brought out a great bowl of punch, but that soon brought them back to a state of warmth and merriment.

---

[10] John Milton (1608-1674) was an English poet and intellectual best known for his 1667 epic poem *Paradise Lost*.

[11] Homer (c. 8th century BC) was a Greek poet credited as the author of the *Iliad* and the *Odyssey*, two epic poems that are foundational works of ancient Greek literature.

A fine carouse[12] the fellows had and when I proposed to lead a party to climb Mount Erebus next day, everyone volunteered to go and my only difficulty was in making a selection. I chose three of the hardiest and the next morning with rubber boots reaching to our waists and so wrapped in woolens that we might pass a night without harm, (if we could but get above the ice and water,) we lowered a boat and pulled into the shelving beach, taking along an extra crew to carry the boat back to the vessel. Laying our boat alongside the ice, we had no difficulty in effecting a landing, as the water was quite smooth and in many places we could easily step out on the ice.

To my surprise, I found the ascent less difficult than I expected. Picking out the easiest ways and keeping as much as possible out of the water, we reached a secondary cone or summit about two-thirds of the way up as darkness, or rather the twilight of the Antarctic night, closed in upon us. The surface was quite dry and warm and I never spent a more comfortable night in these frozen regions than on this lofty peak of Mount Erebus. Getting under a ledge of rocks that sheltered us from the wind, which cut like a knife, we slept soundly without fear of mice or bedbugs. That night we witnessed the grandest display of the aurora australis[13] that perhaps any human eyes ever looked upon before. We were eight or nine thousand feet above the sea, and the luminous bands of purple and orange colored light seemed to spring up from all around us and as they spread toward the zenith and then dipped umbrella shaped to the horizon, the white desolation of this frozen world was suffused with supernatural glory. As we looked out and away on the endless panorama of crags and cliffs and peaks of what seemed to be mountain ranges below us. All deathly white in this unearthly light, it looked

---

[12] A lively and merry drinking party.

[13] An aurora, also commonly known as the polar lights, is a natural light display in Earth's sky, predominantly seen in high-latitude regions. In the north, it is called aurora borealis or Northern Lights, and in the south it is aurora australis or Southern Lights.

ch. ends p. 17

like the ghost of a dead world. The scene was overpowering and after a hasty survey, we were glad to clamber down into our little gorge, out of the uncanny light and smoke our pipes, and hear each other's voices, to bring us back, as it were, to ourselves. This volcano is on the coast of Victoria Land[14] and in all probability we were the first human beings who ever set foot on it. It is between 70 and 80 degrees south latitude and looking east or west as far as the eye could see, with the exception of the stairway like slope tip which we had climbed, stretched an unbroken wall of ice. Looking southward though, with the aid of a glass, I could plainly see an open sea very much like that on the north and clearer of ice. I studied the situation carefully. Here was the impenetrable ice barrier that had baffled every explorer of these southern seas. All below this latitude was supposed to be a continent of ice and snow. Men had sailed down here and been dashed against this wall or had gone back dismayed. But here on the south was the open sea which, if it could be reached, offered to the curious navigator opportunity to go, heaven only knew where. The more I looked at that great open sea. The more I became convinced that there was a passage somewhere through the icy wall connecting these two bodies of water.

We made the descent without incident, and I instructed Captain Brent to hold a safe distance from the ice and circumnavigate the entire Antarctic Circle or find a passage through the ice. Fully imbued then with the idea that the earth was a sphere, I supposed that this body of water on the south was simply an open polar sea, surrounded by walls of ice.

The next day it came on to blow a gale of sleet and snow and we fought northward for four days through such a storm as can only rage in the frozen seas about the South Pole. During these entire four days it was so dark that we could not see the topmast

---

[14]　Victoria Land is a region in eastern Antarctica which fronts the western side of the Ross Sea and the Ross Ice Shelf. It was discovered by Captain James Clark Ross (1800-1862) in January 1841 and named after Queen Victoria (1819-1901).

from the deck though every spar and shroud was white with ice. Several times, we were in dangerous proximity to icebergs, but standing to windward as we were, we could smell the mighty monsters though we could not see them, and keep away. This "smell" of an iceberg, as it is called by seamen, is the peculiar crispness of the air blowing over one of these great bodies of ice and may be felt for miles. The vessel was awash from capstan[15] to wheel,[16] and though we could carry scarcely more canvas[17] than would give us steerage way, her lee scuppers[18] were most of the time dragging through the hissing brine and it was absolutely necessary for every man above deck to lash himself to the rigging to keep from being washed overboard. Cooking was out of the question and for four days there was no fire in the cook's galley, our diet during this time consisting of sea biscuit and tinned food with an occasional pannikin[19] of rum to keep up the warmth. It was a fearful time and though we had encountered much heavy weather on the voyage, we had experienced nothing comparable with this. Indeed, Captain Brent said afterward, that in all his twenty years of voyaging in these waters he had never passed through so terrible a gale.

Only the staunchness of our ship and the skill and experience of our skipper saved us from destruction. It may not be irreverent or presumptuous in me also to feel that an over-ruling Providence guided us through this ice strewn and storm whipped sea, that the great results of our voyage might be achieved.

When the terrific storm subsided and the atmosphere cleared so that we could again see about us, the towering ice

---

[15] A windlass (a type of winch) rotated in a horizontal plane around a vertical axis; used on ships for weighing anchor or raising heavy sails, and typically found on the bow (or front end) of a ship.

[16] A vessel's propeller or paddle-wheel, typically found at the stern (or rear) of a ship.

[17] Open sails.

[18] Openings in the side of a ship at deck level that allow water to drain overboard. Lee indicates that they are partially covered.

[19] A small pan or cup, usually of tin.

ch. ends next p.

barriers were nowhere to be seen. How much northing we had made it was impossible for us to tell as we had entirely lost our reckoning. Heading southward again until we raised the ice wall along which we had been coasting before the gale, we shaped our course parallel to it and held on with the view of finding a passage through it, if there was such a thing.

Fourteen days after this, during which time we encountered all sorts of weather, (for there are never many days together in these seas without a wild snort of wind and snow from some direction,) Captain Brent called me up from my cabin and handing me his glass directed my attention to an opening in the wall of ice before us. Two crystal promontories jutted out into the water on either hand and between, a narrow but well-defined and opened strait. We could not see through, as it was sinuous, [20] but after observing it for some time, we could perceive by the loose ice that was floating about the mouth that a current set into it.

I instantly gave directions to have the vessel headed into this strait. In vain Captain Brent remonstrated and declared that we must be lost if we encountered an ice pack or were overtaken by a storm in this narrow place. "The wind is fair," said he, "but if we encountered an ice pack blocking the passage as we most likely shall we can never navigate the ship out again without more sea room."

It was the first serious disagreement we had ever had since we started on the voyage, and I could not but feel that as navigator, with the responsibility for the safety of the vessel and the lives of the crew, he was right. I begged him though to lay in as close as he could to the mouth of this strait, that we might examine it more closely and on this we compromised and put the vessel's head in toward the opening, intending to heave

---

[20] Winding; having many curves and turns.

to and claw off the shore,[21] as the wind was light and the sea comparatively calm.

And here it did seem that Providence was furthering my apparently wild purpose; for when he had dropped the ship into within a few hundred feet of the opening and ordered the helm down to bring her about, the wind suddenly failed so that there was not steerage way enough to bring the vessel's head around and we drifted helplessly at the mercy of the waves. Instantly all was commotion, for a ship on a shore without wind is in as perilous condition as a steamer with a broken wheel. The bow anchor was quickly cleared and the lead cast, but there was no bottom and so to cast anchor would be useless. The current had now caught us and there was nothing for it but to head straight into the opening, or be broken to pieces on the icy promontories that stood out like Scylla and Charybdis on either hand.[22] My heart bounded as we passed between the towering ice walls, and I felt a thrill of excitement such as Columbus must have experienced when the long looked for Antilles lifted on his expectant vision.[23]

---

[21] "Claw off" is a nautical term meaning to sail away from an area into the wind, typically in a zigzag course.

[22] In Greek Mythology, and depending on which myth referenced, Scylla and Charybdis were sea monsters who occupied opposites sides of the Strait of Messina (a narrow strait between the eastern tip of Sicily and the western tip of Calabria in Southern Italy) and devoured sailors when they tried to navigate it. From the myth grew the idiom "between Scylla and Charybdis," which means being forced to choose between two similarly dangerous situations.

[23] The Antilles is an archipelago, forming the greater part of the West Indies, bordered by the Caribbean Sea to the south and west, the Gulf of Mexico to the northwest, and the Atlantic Ocean to the north and east.

CHAPTER 3

The apprehensions of Captain Brent proved groundless. The passage was open and though there was considerable floating ice, the current was driving it in the same direction and we experienced no difficulty in sailing through. Indeed it was impossible for us to do anything but go through, for after we had gotten fairly into the strait the current was like a mighty, swift, flowing river and had there been a fair wind to go back it must have blown half a gale to drive us against such a tide as was sweeping through. I was convinced that this was a permanent strait and not merely an accidental break in the great barriers. The regular smoothness of the sides showed the effects of a continuous current and the abrasions of great masses of ice carried through by it. I say I was convinced then; but when on our return we found the passage in every respect practically in the same condition as when we passed through first, there was positively no room for doubt. I will not contend that this strait is always open, but I do maintain that it is a permanent channel through which a strong current flows and I am certain that there is a backbone of terra firma underneath these barriers of ice, through which this passage cuts and is as permanent and clearly defined as the straits of Magellan or Gibraltar.

I have a theory, but as it must be elucidated in dry deductions of scientific reasoning, I will not inject it into this narrative. It is my intention though, as soon as possible to prepare a more elaborate work, which I am constrained to believe will be a valuable addition to scientific literature.

It is probable that this passage is sometimes closed by ice packs or the entrance may be jammed with great masses of drift ice, while beyond, the channel may still be open. With a current always flowing through from the north, it is easy to imagine that a great iceberg happening to be nearby would be drawn in. If it were large enough to fill up the passage as many of them are, it would be firmly held there until crushed and broken up by the waves, hiding the strait and giving the appearance of a solid ice wall. Then too, mariners in these wild sea wastes are very cautious, seldom approaching near enough to the barriers to detect this passage even if it were open. What the depth of it is we had no means of ascertaining, for though we spliced together all the lead lines aboard the ship, we never succeeded in finding bottom anywhere.

On account of the tremendous current that set through with the ship, the log was valueless, but from close observation, both going and coming, Captain Brent estimates the length of the passage to be about twenty-five miles. On the farther side the ice walls and sea presented practically the same features as on this, the shining cliffs running away as far as the eye could see on either hand, while the black ocean heaved with great billows that broke with continuous thunder against the barriers or threw their spray high up on the great solemn icebergs that floated in silent majesty, too immense to be shaken by Neptune[1] in the wildest efforts of his wrath.

The sun, which had been rising but a little way above the horizon for some time past, disappeared entirely soon after we got into the open sea beyond the barriers, but when the air was not filled with sleet or snow, it was never really dark. The aurora

---

[1] In Roman Mythology, the god of water and the sea. His Greek equivalent is Poseidon.

australis too, frequently lighted the sea with its weird strange glow so that it was easy for us to keep the frozen coastline in view. My object was now to circumnavigate this polar sea. Sailing eastward along the south side of the barriers until we again came in view of Mount Erebus far off to the northwest, we then headed the ship due south and soon sunk the ice bound coast and mountain beneath the black horizon of the Antarctic Sea.

My idea then was that we were in an open polar sea, ice locked all around and we thought to sail directly across until we reached the barriers on the opposite side and thus obtain a knowledge of its extent.

Shortly after we crossed the ice barriers, the needle became erratic; deflecting more and more every day until it entirely reversed itself. The weather was fair and we detected this by the constellations or we would undoubtedly have sailed out of our course and turned the ship around in following the compass. For weeks after we passed through "Barrington Strait" (as I have been egotistical enough to christen it) we had storms, snow, and ice and the black ocean through which we plowed was in no wise different from that which extends from Cape Horn[2] to Victoria Land, except that we noticed less ice and met with no storms as severe as we encountered on this side, both going and coming. I will not weary the reader with the details of our long voyage in this hitherto unknown ocean. In the course of time, the sun again appeared and as we drew southward, the sea became cleared of ice and the cold moderated as it does in traveling from the poles to the equator. In vain, we looked for the ice barriers, which we supposed surrounded us: only the black open sea stretched on and we held our course. There were no exciting incidents and four months after passing the barriers, we were sailing in open seas out of the region of ice and snow with the weather constantly growing warmer. Two

---

[2] The southernmost headland of the Tierra del Fuego archipelago of southern Chile, notorious for its storms and, until the opening of the Panama Canal in 1914, constituted the only sea route between the Atlantic and Pacific oceans.

ch. ends next p.

months later, we encountered driftwood and not long afterward, sea fowls appeared and grew more numerous every day. They first appeared on the starboard side,[3] and as their number increased from day to day including some that were unmistakably land birds, I expressed the opinion to Captain Brent that we were sailing parallel to some coast and suggested that the ship's course be altered to make this shore. This was done and evidences of land such as seaweed and driftwood became more apparent every day.

My interest and excitement became so great that I could not be still a moment when awake and could sleep but little. In a fever of restlessness, I walked the deck hour after hour and scanned the horizon for land (a perfectly useless waste of energy, as a man was stationed in the lookout, who of course would see the land long before it became visible from the deck.) The weather was fine and we were evidently nearing land of some kind.

As night closed on the 20th of July, an, illumination of some kind was plainly visible on the horizon off the starboard bow and the vessel's head was turned toward it. My excitement was so great that I did not go down to my cabin for supper. The illumination grew plainer constantly and at ten o'clock, the lookout at the masthead said he could distinguish what seemed to be electric lights. At this my hopes fell. I had been thrilled with the idea of approaching an unknown land in an unknown ocean, and now it seemed that in some way we had gotten back into the beaten track of the world and was approaching a modern city. Captain Brent was of the opinion that it was one of the cities on the west coast of South America, although it was impossible to understand how we could have gotten there as we had been sailing south by the heavens ever since we left the polar regions. In a short time, it was plainly to be seen from the deck that we were approaching a considerable

---

[3] On a ship, when facing the bow (or forward), starboard is the right side.

city, lighted by electricity. As we neared the land the lead was heaved constantly and after running in as close as he dared, the captain cast anchor and waited for daylight before attempting to enter the harbor.

As soon as the ship was made snug and everything became quiet on board, I was struck by the strange silence of the city that lay before us. Although evidently a large city and a modern one, (if we might judge from the brilliant manner in which it was lighted,) there was an entire absence of that roar and rumble which characterizes the modern American or European city. As a matter of fact, although we lay within a few miles, no sound of any kind came to us and the silence was strange and weird-like, as though it was some brilliantly illuminated city of the dead.

CHAPTER 4

I was awakened next morning by the creaking of the winch and the rattling of the cable as the anchor was hoisted and, dressing hurriedly, I went on deck where the captain and crew were discussing the small craft that was coming out of the harbor. Even as we looked, a most remarkable boat came tearing out and pitching toward us at the rate of at least fifty miles an hour. As it came toward us, we could see only a great billow of foam and above it a covered deck something like a ferryboat or excursion barge. When it came alongside of us, we could see that the vessel (if such a thing may be called a vessel), consisted of a long cigar shaped hull submerged after the fashion of the American whaleback,[1] with the superstructure raised on stanchions.[2] On each end of this cylindrical hull were great cone-shaped screws somewhat larger than the hull itself, and it was these that raised the billows of foam as they leaped through the water, pushing and dragging the strange looking boat. A uniformed pilot was put aboard, and a towing hawser[3] thrown to the men in the bow. Saluting and speaking perfect English, though with a peculiar accent, the pilot asked what vessel it was. On being

---

[1] A thing that is shaped like a whale's back.
[2] Upright or vertical posts or supports.
[3] A thick rope or cable for mooring or towing a ship.

informed that it was the *Wanderer* of New York, United States of America, he dropped his jaw, stretched his eyes, and looked altogether as upset as if he had been told that it was the Flying Dutchman.[4]

"What land is this?" asked Captain Brent in turn.

"The Iron Republic, sir," replied the pilot, again saluting, and advancing to the wheel. In response to our further questioning, he courteously stated that he was an officer on duty, that it was against the rules for him to hold any conversation except in reference to the ship and begged us to curb our curiosity until we got ashore, when all the information we desired would be afforded us.

There was nothing else for us to do, so Captain Brent turned his attention to lowering and furling the sails, which had been hoisted, and by the time everything was made snug, we were alongside the pier.

As soon as we were made fast another officer came on board and he, like the pilot, seemed to be dumbfounded when he learned that the vessel hailed from the United States of America. After inspecting the ship's papers, he turned to Captain Brent and informed him that the circumstances of our arrival were so unusual and unprecedented in his experience that he would be under the necessity of conducting him to the office of the Director of Navigation. Thereupon, the captain introduced me as owner and the proper person to deal with, and the officer politely requested me to accompany him.

"Sir," said I, as we passed through the curious throng that had gathered on the wharf, "will you be kind enough to tell me what country this is and in what part of the world it lies?"

"This," he replied, "is the Iron Republic and the continent on which you stand lies about as far from the frozen ocean as your own continent of America does in the opposite direction."

Just here, having reached the outskirts of the crowd, he made

---

[4] The Flying Dutchman is a legendary ghost ship, allegedly never able to make port, but doomed to sail the seven seas forever.

a signal, and a man approached with a horseless vehicle and, dismounting, saluted and opened the door of his carriage. Forbearing to question further an officer of whose power and authority I had not the slightest idea, and whose extreme courtesy forbade impertinence, I took my place in the carriage and was whirled along wide, smooth streets through the heart of the city. I have remarked that though we lay just outside of the harbor and in sight of the city for some hours before entering, we heard none of that roar and rumble inseparable from cities of its apparent size among us. The reason was now plain. In the first place, the streets were all as smooth as a tennis court and there was nothing to make a noise. There was not a horse to be seen and it was evident from the floor-like cleanliness of the streets that they were not intended for the use of horses and wagons. On all sides were horseless vehicles of every description, from the lightest bicycles to large covered vans, all rubber tired, whirling to and fro swiftly and without noise.

I had only time to note the things referred to and to remark the strange and picturesque costumes of the ladies and gentlemen who were on the street, when my conductor drew up before a large substantial stone building covering an entire block. Stepping down from the carriage, he assisted me to alight and ushered me into a large and well-lighted reception room in the front of the building. I noticed as we approached that a blue flag with a white star floated from the tower on the roof, and surmised that in some way the two officers with whom I had been brought in contact and the building, which we had just entered, represented the same department of government.

Conducting me to one of the comfortable seats with which the room was supplied, my companion excused himself by saying that the gentleman who met me at the boat would be with me in a few minutes and withdrew. Scarcely had he passed through the door when the person deferred to came in, having presumably ridden up after us in his own carriage. Smiling pleasantly, he expressed the hope that I would not be

ch. ends p. 35

annoyed by the little conventionalities to which I was being subjected, saying that my arrival was so extraordinary and so out of common with all other entries made since he had been connected with the marine, that he had no other recourse but to refer me to the head of the department. I assured him that I was under obligations for his courteous attention; that a stranger as I was and dazed by the extraordinary circumstances in which I found myself, I was in a condition to absolutely require guidance and direction.

He desired me to consider myself under no restraint whatever, stating that I was being referred to the chief of the Bureau of Navigation, because he was at a loss to know how to place me on the marine register. Opening a door, he conducted me without ceremony into the presence of a gentleman whom he introduced as "Director of Navigation and Chief of the Department of the Marine." This officer, notwithstanding his evident high position, rose and smiling cordially bowed and asked us both to be seated. In a few words the subordinate explained to his superior the circumstances of my arrival and asked for instructions in certain matters pertaining to the registering of my vessel. These were given and then the high official with rare feeling and tact arose and grasped my hand and welcomed me to the Iron Republic; saying that though it might lack the associations which must make my native country pleasant, it possessed advantages and attractions which he believed, from what he had been able to learn, could not be found in America. I thanked him for his cordial greeting and assured him that while some associations of my own country had been pleasant, others were very unpleasant and upon the whole, I was glad to have found my way to the "Iron Republic," whatever and wherever it might be.

After inquiring into the details of my voyage in which he manifested great interest, the director remarked that the astonishment of his countrymen at my arrival would naturally be much less than mine, inasmuch as they had a very thorough knowledge of my country. It was known, he said, from the settlement of his country that the American continent existed; indeed that it was the attempt of a ship load of emigrants to get to America that led to the discovery of the continent on which the magnificent structure of government known as the Iron Republic had been reared. This was in 1698, and driven southward by fierce gales the colonists after many months of battling with storm and ice, found themselves cast on the inhospitable shores of a new world. For many years after the first settlement was made, it was supposed by the colonists that they were on a portion of the American continent, but with the development of the country, the increase of knowledge, and the researches of navigators, it was found that they had been discoverers as well as colonizers. They knew all that was known in Europe of the American continent up to the time they were so effectually cut off from the balance of the civilized world and within the past fifty years two other American ships had drifted to their shores. When I told him how many lives had been lost and how much treasure had been squandered by America and other nations in Arctic explorations, and expressed surprise that a people so advanced in the arts of civilization as his nation appeared to be, should make no attempts to establish communication with other parts of the world, but should remain isolated for centuries, he smiled pleasantly and said he could appreciate my feelings.

In the first place, he explained that the Iron Republic had never been engaged in maritime commerce to any considerable extent even in the days when trading was encouraged, as there were no other great maritime nations to trade with, as a consequence there was not that passion for voyaging and exploration, which obtains among a maritime people. Nevertheless, some attempts had been made to get through the barriers and as vessels had sailed away and never returned, it was supposed at the time that some of them might have succeeded in the attempt. Since the establishment of the great republic though, no efforts

ch. ends p. 35

had been made in that direction for the reason that there was not sufficient private capital to undertake such enterprises and from the knowledge they had of the outside world, the government did not desire closer intercourse with the older nations as it could not possibly do them any good and might result in much harm. This, he admitted, was a species of national selfishness; "but selfishness," said he, with a smile, "is human and is one thing we have in common with all peoples past and present." He then told me that a Captain Morris had reached their country with a ship and crew during the progress of the great civil war and that some years before that an old American whaler had come to their shores. The whaler remained with them a year and then left with the intention of making his way back to America and was never heard of again. Captain Morris, he informed me, was then in the country and being a man of great ability was at the head of the government Naval College. Most of his crew, too, were still living and were established in different parts of the country.

At the conclusion of an hour of pleasant conversation, the affable Director touched a button, saying that it was very probable that the press had given out the details of my arrival. Speaking into a bell-shaped transmitter directly over his table he called "current news," and then pushed back his chair in a listening attitude.

In a moment, a voice, rich, strong, and distinct, answered back through the transmitter:

"Current news!—Eight o'clock to ten—President Wilkes and party arrived this morning at 8:20 by the through express, making the 760 miles from the capital to Corinthus in four hours and ten minutes. The president comes down to participate in the formal opening of the new Temple this evening. Everything is in perfect readiness and when the lights are turned on tonight the people will have no cause to regret the money expended in its construction. It will seat 5,000 people and the architects, Messrs. Horn & Jamison, claim for it the most perfect acoustic qualities of any auditorium in the Republic except possibly the amphitheater of the capital. In tests made yesterday, a whisper on the platform could be heard with perfect distinctness in the third gallery. The grand harmonium has been furnished with another chime of bells, the first set having been rejected by Prof. Hallam on account of defectiveness of tone. 'The Winter King,' Churchill's last masterpiece, will be rendered for the first time tonight. Prof. Hallam has pronounced it one of the greatest triumphs of the musical art. As the demand for seats will be large, admission will be had by drawings commencing promptly at 12:30 p.m. No change of program as given.

"Senator Cromwell, of the Province of Urbana had an attack of paralysis this morning at 6 o'clock as he was plowing in his field and has not yet recovered consciousness. This is his second attack and the physicians fear it may prove fatal. Senator Cromwell is in the fourth year of his office as representative of the great province of Urbana and, by his modest dignity and usefulness, has made himself one of the most popular senators that ever filled the office. He was the inventor of the Cromwell harrow and was the first to adopt the practice of dehorning cattle.

"Exchange reports show that 27 million diems were canceled yesterday. This large volume of business was caused by the approaching cooler weather, which called out a heavy tonnage of coal. Potatoes in bond are not doing well and the Bureau of Subsistence has ordered them cut 20 percent to encourage consumption and prevent loss.

"The sensation of the day is the arrival at the port of Corinthus of another vessel from America. It was brought

ch. ends p. 35

up this morning about 8 o'clock and is a typical American ship of 250 tons. Capt. Brent, master, with a crew of eight. The vessel is owned by J. Edward Barrington of the United States and sailed through the barriers about seven months ago. Mr. Barrington is at present in conference with the Director of Navigation and it is not known what his plans for the future are.

"A great crowd has already collected on the pier and Prof. Morris, the well-known American author and president of the Naval College, will arrive from the capital on the 12 o'clock express to meet his countryman.

"Special resume at 12 o'clock."

The voice ceased and touching the button again, the director turned to me. I have not given all or anything like half what came to us as current news, but just simply a sample. I inquired if this news was being read from a daily paper through the telephone and the director replied that it was the paper (or what corresponded to it) itself.

"Do you mean to say," I asked with astonishment, "that all of the people get the news as we have just heard it?"

"I mean to say," answered the director, "that several millions of people heard or had the opportunity of hearing the same voice, giving out the same news that we have just listened to."

"And there is no paper printed?" I asked, scarcely able to grasp the idea of such a news service.

"None except what is printed right there," pointing to a small machine I had noticed ticking on the table. "Every word you have heard is reproduced there in print and can be preserved for future reading or destroyed at the option of the patron."

I stepped to the table and looked, but could make nothing of the cabalistic[5] signs on the paper before me. "How is it,"

---

[5] Having a secret or hidden meaning.

I inquired, "that you speak the English language and do not use the Roman characters as other English speaking people do?"

"We used the same letters," answered the director, "until the discovery of sound characters. Most of our books are printed in the old way, only the newest literature being printed with the sound characters."

"What do you call a sound character?" I asked.

"I may not be able to make you understand," said the director, "if you are unfamiliar with the development and progress of the knowledge of sound."

I told him that the nature of sound as atmospheric vibrations was well understood by us and mentioned the telephone and phonograph in common use as an illustration.

"Very well then," said he, "it is simple enough. The vibrations are communicated to the machine and the machine transmutes them into characters. Reproduce a sound a million times and it will make the same character every time. It is a true phonetic system and is Nature's own writing."

Amazed at a civilization evidently so far in advance of ours. I had forgotten the circumstances by which I was surrounded and would have questioned further, but the genial official excused himself, saying that his duties would deprive him of the further pleasure of my company at that time, but that he hoped to meet me again soon, outside of business hours and in a social way. In the meantime, I would receive the attention of the government. Pressing another button, he informed me that a carriage was ready to return me to my vessel, where in a few hours I would probably be called upon by my distinguished countryman and other representatives of the government.

Grasping his extended hand heartily I thanked him for his kindness and returned to the wharf.

As I approached, in the conduct of the same officer who had carried me from the boat, the curious crowd fell back respectfully and I passed on board. Notwithstanding our position was one calculated to repress every emotion except astonishment,

ch. ends next p.

I found Captain Brent in a tremendous state of wrath and the steward was describing the heathenish country to which we had drifted, in a flight of profanity that was positively eloquent. On learning the cause, I found that the last named dignitary had been out in the city trying to purchase fresh meats and vegetables, of which the men stood in great need after their long voyage. It seemed though; that neither gold or silver would be accepted in payment and so the dinner of fresh victuals[6] that all had looked forward to so eagerly, was not in sight. We were soon relieved, however, by the appearance of a van load of fresh supplies, which the vendor said was brought on an order from the Marine office.

I retired to my cabin and tried to collect my thoughts. I had been but a few hours in this wonderful country and already my senses had taken in more, it seemed to me, than my mind could analyze and digest in weeks. I felt as if I would like to get away by myself for two or three days and think it over. Everything was so new and strange, that all mental effort was directed to grasping the situation.

After a dinner of fresh meats and vegetables, the first we had tasted since we left America, I was called on by Prof. Morris, a fine looking gentleman, apparently about sixty-five years old, who came aboard with the burgomaster[7] of the city and several other persons of position, and welcomed us all to the Iron Republic. Our countryman seemed delighted to see us and he was to me the one link that connected us with a former world and imparted reality to scenes and circumstances that would otherwise have seemed an illusion. After an hour's conversation in which the voyage was discussed and in which I learned that he had come through the barriers by the same channel that we had, he left us saying that he would call in the evening and take Captain Brent and myself to the opening of

[6] Food or provisions.

[7] The principal magistrate, comparable to a mayor, of a Dutch, Flemish, German, Austrian, or Swiss city or town.

the new temple where we would have the opportunity to see the president and meet him afterward.

Prof. Morris was of the same opinion as myself in regard to the permanency of the strait which brought us through the barriers, but he thought it probable that it might be gorged with ice and remain closed for years at a time.

Indeed, he thought that it was perhaps only open at rare intervals when the seas were unusually clear of ice. However that may be, I found the strait open both going and coming and, except for the current, experienced no difficulty whatever in getting through, and it is my opinion, based on a theory which I have formed and which will be fully explained in my forthcoming book, that there is yet another passage through these barriers which may be found if it is sought for with half the ardor that has been devoted to Arctic explorations.

CHAPTER 5

We accompanied Prof. Morris to witness the opening of the new temple that evening and as we took our places in the tier of seats set apart for visitors and strangers, I never gazed upon a finer interior or saw a more superior audience. From pit to gallery was such an array of female toilets[1] as was never dreamed of in America. Indeed, it seemed to me, as my eyes swept over the magnificent auditorium, some grand pageant prepared in honor of a royal Mardi Gras or fête.[2] The costumes of the ladies were similar in style and richness to those of the most superb ballet and every gentleman was in full dress with knee breeches, ruffles, and buttoner. What seemed remarkable to me was that the people in the last gallery were just as handsomely dressed as any in the house. I called Prof. Morris' attention to this and he informed me that there were no social differences in any part of the house; that the seats were all drawn by lot and the most distinguished person in the city might draw a seat in the gallery, while a hod carrier[3] got the best in the house. As a matter of

[1] In this context: attire or dress; meaning female dresses.
[2] Festival or celebration.
[3] A hod is a trough used for transporting loads, usually bricks or mortar, and carried over the shoulder.

fact he said it would be difficult to make social distinctions, as the President of the Republic was a brick mason.

Just then the orchestra, or rather the great Harmonium, began to play and the laughter and conversation of the brilliant assemblage drowned in a crash of music, grander than anything I had ever heard before. From a tremendous explosion of harmony, it would sink to the softest tones of flute and harp and then again swell to a crash of melodious sounds in which were chimes of deep toned bells, roar of drums, shrieking of horns, and concussion of anvils, dying away again to the delicate tremulous quaver of a single violin string. And as these divine strains from the instrument rose and fell in the production of the musical drama, the theme was illustrated by wonderful spectacular view projected on the curtain of the stage. I noticed from the program that this production was the "Winter King," and as the fierce north wind howled and shrieked and moaned in the musical passages, the snow fell in the spectacular and the sleet-laden trees crashed before the blast. Anon, [4] breakers boomed and thundered on a rockbound shore and then could be seen a dismantled ship drifting to wreck and ruin. Altogether, it was the grandest thing I ever saw, or, it seemed to me, that human genius could produce. Another fine effect I noticed was produced by the electric lights set in the dome-shaped ceiling. These lights were covered by partly colored glass globes that at intervals revolved, throwing every shade of beautiful light over the audience with changing and shifting tints weirdly beautiful. The intention of this, I surmised, was to heighten the illusion by thus eliminating the audience, making it as strangely unreal as possible. It was successful and, in all, beautiful beyond my powers of description. You not only heard, you saw and felt. With the dying away of the last deep roll of thunder, the sinking of the wind to a sighing zephyr, the subsidence of the black, white-manned sea, the sweet warbling of a bird that seemed

---

[4] In a short time; soon.

to carol its song in an ecstasy of delight that nature's convulsion was passed, the grand finale was reached, the sun burst forth as if by magic, the great auditorium was illuminated by a pure white light, bright as day, and then the curtain rose. As it rolled up a picture was seen in the background, at the sight of which the concourse of five thousand people rose as one man and waved their handkerchiefs and applauded to the top of their bent.[5] It was a simple picture and yet it evoked the wildest enthusiasm. Just a backing of sky and in the foreground a massive iron pillar with a quality of solidity and inertia about it, which no words can convey. Overarching the pillar was a rainbow and on it were inscribed the words, "The State Was Made For Man. Not Man For The State." On the pillar was the statute of a man with a hammer poised and above it floated a blue flag with a white star in the center. This was the device[6] of the Iron Republic and certainly, if enthusiasm proves anything, it was a loyal audience.

When the cheering finally subsided a rather stout, awkward looking gentleman walked out on the stage and was received with an ovation. He appeared to be young, though prematurely bald, and so timid that it was not until after several efforts that he succeeded in finding his voice. When he did, he introduced another gentleman, tall and handsome, as "Prof. Churchill, the author of the 'Winter King' and an artist whom we all delight to honor." The artist received his need of applause and bowing with a gratified smile they both left the platform.

"Ah," said I turning to Prof. Morris, "now I perceive that I am indeed in the Iron Republic, for your Churchill would never have gotten off in American without a speech."

"Never fear," replied my companion, "we will doubtless have speeches enough before we are through, even in the Iron Republic."

On inquiring who the timid young man was that appeared

---

[5] In this context: propensity or inclination.
[6] In this context: emblem or heraldic design.

ch. ends p. 42

on the stage first and was received with such applause, I was informed that it was Prof. Hallam of the National Conservatory and the greatest musician in the Republic. After this incident, a fine looking gentleman advanced to the center of the stage in front of the picture, bearing a silver shield on which rested a massive key of gold. I was somewhat startled at this lavishness, but I was to learn to my cost, that gold in that country was a vastly different thing from gold in other parts of the world.

Walking to front, the gentleman spoke as follows:

"Fellow citizens. I have the honor to present to you through your executive this evening, the keys to this edifice, which is to be consecrated to the education, elevation, and happiness of our race. Its foundations are of granite, its walls of marble, its roof of glass and phosphor-bronze—imperishable materials, as becomes the temple of an imperishable nation. It is not a monument of dead stones to cover the bones of dead oppressors as are the granite heaps of Egypt and of Rome, but a living temple made animate by the spirit of art, philosophy, and religion, of which it is to be the concrete body. Its dust may fly on the winds of future ages or fructify[7] the fields of those to whom we will be an ancient race, but virtue is immortal and the noble passions and ambitions kindled here will live forever, beyond the remorseless touch of time. Fellow citizens, I deliver to you that which is yours and relinquish all right and claim to it whatever!"

Here a modest looking gentleman with stooping shoulders and the carriage of a working man mounted the platform amid perfect tumult of applause and, lifting the key from the shield with a bow, thanked the architect (for such he was), in a few well-chosen words, for the skill and painstaking bestowed in the creation of such a work of art; and as that gentleman retired from the stage, turned to the audience and spoke in part as follows: "Fellow citizens. The earth may be likened to a great

---

[7] Make productive or fruitful.

laboratory where things are made, tested, and improved, and where nothing is perfect enough, as yet, to be stamped with the seal of immortality. So far, eternal power seeks no permanent form. Changeless in its nature, it is most changeful in its manifestations and expresses itself in a million forms that wax and wane and pass away, leaving the spirit of power to enter other bodies. Under the dust of the moist-less desert we find the track of the long perished river. Beneath the greenest landscape, lie other landscape buried. So in the realm of thought. Delve where we may, in literature, art, philosophy, or religion, we evermore turn up the ashes of things that were; and so in turn, shall the dust of things which are, slip through Time's fingers and find the roofs of things to be.

"And as genius molds and remolds the pliant clay till the perfect form is reached; as the eagle with each revolution in his circling flight mounts upward to the sun, so Nature, in her ceaseless evolutions grows more perfect with each succeeding change. The earth-born wrestler in the Greek mythology was thrown down but sprang up, strengthened by contact with his mother Earth! And so death levels all, only that life may spring up in new and more perfect forms.

"The awful mystery of life and death, of darkness and light, of good and evil, we may not understand; but, we know that where two lions matched strength to strength and died in combat, sprang up two lilies fragrant and fair; and enriched by the dead carcasses of savage beasts they grew luxuriantly tall and beautiful. Thus does nature through the mystery of death effect the transmutation of savageness and strength into sweetness and beauty. And thus do her analogies teach us, that the evils and inharmonious of the present time shall combat each other to death and through death transmute their undying forces into harmonious forms of beauty. And so shall the flight of the arrow become the spray of the fountain, the sweep of the broad sword the song of the circling scythe, the tumult of war, the shouting of children at play!"

ch. ends next p.

We give this introduction of the president because it was so fine of itself and so impressive and effective in its simple and modest delivery. In his further remarks, he dwelt on the affairs of the Republic, the prosperity of the people and the possibilities of the future. It was a splendid address of twenty or thirty minutes, after which there was more music, the reading of a poem composed by a local poet for the occasion and an address by the burgomaster. There were also remarks by a celebrated actor and the program closed with a beautiful anthem by Prof. Hallam and an invocation and benediction by a venerable old gentleman who I understood my countryman to say was a Professor of Christian Philosophy. At the conclusion of the exercises, Captain Brent and myself were presented to the president and had a few minutes of pleasant conversation with him. He informed us that he was made aware of our arrival in a few minutes after we came ashore, and would have telephoned his greeting but that he anticipated the pleasure of meeting us in a few hours. He tendered Captain Brent and myself the freedom of the Republic and invited us to accompany him to the capital the next day. The invitation was warmly seconded by Prof. Morris, who commanded us to make his house our home during the visit. Being desirous above all things to see the country, I accepted their invitations and parted from them with the understanding that I should meet them at the office of the affable Director of Navigation the next afternoon.

CHAPTER 6

On our return to the vessel, Captain Brent and myself discussed the situation thoroughly, and decided, so far as the ship was concerned, to leave everything in *statue quo*[1] for the time being. I instructed him to pay the crew up to date and without canceling articles, to give them all shore leave for thirty days with the privilege of going where they pleased in the country or remaining on the vessel at their option. He with the steward was to remain on board.

The next morning I went out to look up a bank with the view of converting some of my gold into money of the realm. Failing to find any such institutions, or even to make anyone understand my wants, I had recourse to my countryman, Prof. Morris, who had been thoughtful enough to give me his address the night before. I informed him of my desire, at which he looked grave and asked me what my resources were. I told him that I had money enough to answer all my present wants, having about $50,000 in American gold in my safe aboard the vessel, and that what I wanted was to find a safe bank where I could deposit it and convert it into money of the country as occasion should require.

[1] Translated from Latin: in the same situation; in the same place.

"My dear sir," said the professor seriously, "I fear your greatest disappointment with the country will be when I enlighten you on the subject of your inquiry. Such things as banks are unknown in the financial system of this country."

"But surely," said I, "there are places of exchange where I can convert American gold into the currency of the country?"

"No," replied he, for the simple reason that gold is not money in this country and is convertible into money on the basis of its intrinsic value, as iron, coal, and other commodities are."

"I understand that," I interrupted, "and in that, your system is not really different from ours. Gold money with us is based on the intrinsic value of the metal and therein differs from silver and other forms of currency. That is the beauty of the gold standard to which the United States is destined. There is no artificial or 'fiat' value inhering in it, consequently it is worth as much in any other country as it is in ours."

"Yes," replied the professor, with a smile, "it is worth as much in any other country where it is used for money, but you must know my dear sir that it is from its use as money, that it derives its chief value. In this country, it is never used for money and its intrinsic value is only what it derives from its utility in other respects the same as tin, iron, or copper. It is not half so useful as any of these, but it is much scarcer and is relatively higher on that account. Still, you must be terribly disappointed when I tell you that what was a handsome fortune for you in America is comparatively an insignificant sum in the Iron Republic. There will not be the slightest trouble though in converting it into money of the realm and you need have no hesitancy about doing it, as you can reconvert it into gold at the same rate any time. In other words, you can deposit it in the government exchange, receiving its value in currency with the privilege of exchanging the currency for gold again at any time. Come," said he, "let us go down and arrange it at once."

Going out we took a kind of horseless cab and soon alighted before, by far, the largest building I had yet seen. Rather I should say we alighted in it, for the streets passed through the building, as did a number of railroads. Going into an office the professor walked up to the counter and asked the price of gold. The clerk in charge handed out an official sheet that looked like a market report and with his pencil pointed to the quotation of gold in the list. We learned from this that it was worth two diems (pronounced dayems) per pound. A simple calculation showed my $50,000 of American coin to be worth about $666. I was dumbfounded. In a single moment, I felt a handsome fortune swept from my hands. I actually cowered as from a blow. My companion must have noted it, for he slapped me on the shoulder and rallied me, saying that I was richer in the Iron Republic without a dollar than I would be anywhere else in the world with a million. "Six hundred dollars! Why," said I despairingly, "that is not enough to support me until I can find work!"

"Why, my friend, that is enough to keep you in comfort for several years. And there is your vessel worth 10,000 diems at least, enough to make you a very rich man indeed in this country."

After ascertaining the market value of my gold, it took but a short time to have it brought to the government exchange and weighed in. Before the metal was weighed in, the clerk in charge asked me for my seal; I in turn looked inquiringly and rather helplessly to Prof. Morris, who explained that I was not a citizen and therefore had no seal. This seemed likely to prove a fatal hitch in the proceedings, for the clerk said it was impossible for him to certify me unless I had a seal. After consultation, it was arranged by having Prof. Morris deposit for me. It may be supposed that I was an interested observer of these conventionalities, so entirely new and strange to me. Drawing what appeared to be a disk of hard rubber about the size of a twenty-five cent piece from his purse, my friend dropped it into the slot of a registering device attached to the scales, the clerk in charge pressed a lever and a small card fell out along with

ch. ends p. 60

the professor's seal, placing the seal in his pocket Prof. Morris handed me the card. On one side was a facsimile of the seal, a circular ornamented border and within these words, "W. A. Morris. American, citizen by grace, 1863." On the reverse was stamped in figures that cut into the card, the exact weight of the metal.

The entire business was transacted without the agent of the government ever touching the gold or the receipt for it. From the scales the metal was passed to the assayer[2] nearby, who put a stamp under the weight, indicating its fineness and then it was tagged and carried to a vault-like storeroom. Passing to another department (for the place was arranged similar to a great bank), the professor laid down his card and had counted out to him a pile of bills something like bank checks, (ruled crossways on the back to hold many signatures), aggregating 654 diems, the alloy in the gold making it worth 12 diems less than the quoted price. These bills were handed over to me and the business was completed. The whole transaction consumed scarcely more time than it takes to describe it and we went from there to the Marine Office where we met the president, and the three of us lunched with the Director of Navigation at a hotel. At two o'clock, we repaired to the station to take the cars for the capital of the Republic. The president and Prof. Morris were recognized and greeted courteously by almost everyone we met, but there was no groveling or sycophancy.[3] I could scarcely realize that I was in the company of the president of a great nation, so simple and unpretentious were his manners and carriage. He carried his own carpetbag in his hand and seemed to expect no more deference than anybody else.

Prof. Morris purchased my ticket for me and we sat down with a number of others in a comfortable waiting room and in a few minutes a porter came in and announced that the "Capital City express" was waiting. We went through a gate where our

---

[2] One who analyzes a metal or ore to determine its quality and components.
[3] Self-seeking flattery.

tickets were taken up and passed into the cars. These cars were four feet wide, six feet high and twenty-four feet long. The seats extended entirely across the car and there was no provision made for walking about in the coach. Between every two seats, placed to face each other, a door opened from the side, so that they were practically compartment cars with room in each compartment for four persons. There were a dozen or fifteen of these cars in the train, but no locomotive engineer or conductor was in sight. I noticed that the end of the car at the front of the train was pointed like the bow of a boat and when the passengers were ushered into the cars, the doors were all locked from the outside. A full description of these railroads with detail drawings and specifications of their entire equipment is furnished with my official report, but will not be injected into this narrative, as it would doubtless be tedious to the lay reader. In order though that my reader may better understand the plan of the cars I have been describing, I will state that this railroad was an elevated affair, massive iron pillars set in the ground like those on which are laid the elevated railroads of New York. There was no heavy superstructure though, as in American elevated railways, the tracks or girders on which the cars run, being placed, one at the top and the other about six feet lower down, thus making one track directly above the other instead of being side by side, as on American railways. The cars were elevated on an average about ten feet from the ground. On account of depressions they sometimes ran considerably higher, but never less than ten feet over a road or lower than six feet anywhere. Thus, they could encounter no obstacles and were so attached to the track that they could not fly off even if the wheels on which they ran were broken or detached. The railway was double tracked, that is there were two sets of tracks, one on either side of the upright iron pillars and the cars on opposite sides, ran in opposite directions, so they could never collide. The columns which supported this novel railway were set about the same distance apart as those of an American elevated

ch. ends p. 60

road and as they took up scarcely any room and required no right of way, the road ran through farms and villages without danger or inconvenience to anybody. The freight cars, of which I saw a great many standing in the government storehouse, or exchange, were simply iron cylinders of about the same size as the passenger cars. The passenger trains were run in the daytime and the freight trains at night. This description applies to all of the railroads in the Republic, except some roads, which were built for carrying coal, ores, etc. These run underground. These roads are run entirely different from American railways, trains never stopping at stations to put off or take on passengers. After it leaves the starting point, a car never stops till its reaches its destination where it is switched down from the main line and rests on a track underneath it and on a level with the floor of the station. For instance, the train we took at Corinthus, never slackened speed a particle from the time it got underway until it ran down on its siding at Ironia, some seven hundred miles distant. No car ever stops on the main line and by a very ingenious arrangement, cars on the main line can never get within less than ten miles of each other. The motive power is electricity and when they get closer together than ten miles, the current is cut off from the rear train so that it loses speed. I have, as I have said, a full technical description of this railway system, furnished me by the government engineer, for it goes without saying that it is owned and managed entirely by the government.

In a few moments after the bustling porter ushered us into our compartment, we started off with a gentle motion which increased until within less than two minutes, we were flying across the country with a velocity I never conceived of before. There was no noise, no jar, the motion being more like that of a flying iceboat or smooth toboggan slide, than anything else. The president and Prof. Morris endeavored to draw me into conversation, but a faintness and dizziness came over me so prostrating that I seemed on the verge of collapse.

I struggled against it and brought to bear all the force of will I possessed, but the fearful speed completely unnerved me. The cars being elevated above the ground and the windows but little below the level of the eye, we could only see the landscape at some distance and as it flew by I felt as if I were imprisoned in a great cannonball being fired through space. Cold perspiration broke out on me and try as I might, it was impossible for me to conceal my distress. It was not fear, for I knew from the construction of the cars and road that an accident was reasonably impossible and I was assured by my companions that a fatal accident had never occurred on the road. It was only the smooth, noiseless, terrible speed that affected me and within an hour it wore off and I was myself again and began to take a lively interest in the country through which we were passing. As we sped on through great tracts of country covered with farms, towns and villages, over great rivers, across hills and valleys, it made a flying panorama beautiful beyond description.

Frequently we intersected other roads like ours with flying cars, crossing either above or below them.

It was not long after I had recovered sufficiently to become interested in the outside world, before I observed what, strangely enough, I had not noticed before. That was people flying about the country with the greatest ease and grace. I had not noticed any suggestion of aerial navigation at Corinthus, but Prof. Morris told me that if I had been in the suburbs, I would have seen hundreds of people out every fine afternoon flying for pleasure.

I was not surprised to see the air navigated, for I had long been of the opinion that it was only a matter of time when the feat would be accomplished in America. I was surprised though at the simplicity of the flying machines. I had been accustomed to think of a practical flying machine as something very complicated and large; a kind of balloon, car, and steamboat combined. But here were people flying about with the greatest ease, with nothing but a sail drawn over a frame like a great bird's wings,

ch. ends p. 60

underneath which they swung like a spider under his web. A propelling wheel of the same materials was driven sometimes by light machinery, but most often by the muscles of the flyers.

It all seemed so easily and gracefully done that I could not help wondering that people were not flying the world over.

"How is it," I asked my companions, "that people here seem to do so easily what we have labored vainly so many years in my country to accomplish? Are you stronger, or is the atmosphere more dense?"

"Neither one nor the other," answered Prof. Morris. "You people have always gone at it the wrong way, or had, up to the time I left the country. You have been swallowed up with the idea of machinery. You have seen birds carry their own weight and twice as much besides, with ease; you have seen clumsy squirrels expand their skins by stretching out their legs and make astonishing flights through the air, and yet though knowing that man is one of the strongest animals in the world to his size, it has not yet occurred to you to apply that strength intelligently in the effort to fly. Really your attempts at flying have been quite as ridiculous as it would be to attempt to swim by machinery! With a light aeroplane having the requisite area of surface and a simple gear with which he could apply the strength of his back, arms, and legs to a propelling fan, your boys, with the opportunity, would learn to fly quite as easily as they learn to swim. All you require to enable 'Young America' to acquire expertness in the air as he does in the water and on the ice is the simple aeroplane and a high wire two or three hundred feet in length from which he could suspend himself while learning to manipulate his flyer."

A moment's reflection convinced me that the professor was right and during the entire trip, nothing interested me so much as to watch the graceful flyers of whom there were nearly always some in view.

I inquired if there were not a very great many casualties resulting from such hazardous exercises and was informed that there were none at all. That if anything should happen to the aeronaut in midair; the aeroplane would let him down to earth as gently as a parachute and without danger. Seeing how absorbed I was with the outside view and appreciating my curiosity, my companions very considerately left me to myself for the most part of the journey, while they discussed matters of interest to the country at large. We arrived at the capital at six o'clock, making the 700 miles in four hours and twenty-five minutes.

When we reached our destination and the train stopped, the doors were opened for the first time since we started and, descending, we found ourselves in a large vaulted room surrounded by all the bustle incident to a great and prosperous city.

Prof. Morris called a carriage and parting from President Wilkes (who cordially invited me to call on him at the executive department), we took our seats and were driven—or propelled rather, through wide tree-bordered streets to the professor's home in the suburbs.

Being but a dull practical clod, language fails me to describe the feelings and impressions of that hour. The streets were brilliantly lighted and were filled with gaily dressed people, some walking, some riding in carriages or on bicycles, some standing in knots about the corners or sitting on rustic iron seats under the trees along the curb, and notwithstanding the great concourse there was no noise except the laughter and conversation of the people. As in Corinthus, there was not a horse to be seen, all of the conveyances being self-propelling. The light and glamor, the beautiful costumes, the noiseless, swiftly moving carriages all seemed like a dream of fairyland.

In the delightful home of my countryman and patron, there was not so much to remind me that I was in a strange country. The decorations and furnishings were not so different from that of the best houses in America, except that besides real works of art there seemed to be a strict adherence to the rule that everything that was there was there for use. There was no piling

ch. ends p. 60

up of heterogeneous and conglomerate masses of trumpery such as is to be found in many so-called fashionable houses of America under the general term of bric-a-bac. The general style of furnishing was something between American luxuriousness and Japanese simplicity and utility.

The room into which I was ushered seemed to be a parlor, library, and general receiving room all in one and was warmed by electricity, but that cheerful glow which the sight of a ruddy fire imparts was obtained by having an open grate piled with inconsumable fagots[4] that blazed white and red when the current was turned on. A handsome instrument reaching almost to the ceiling (and which I afterward found to be a combination pipe organ and grand piano,) stood in one corner and by it, a music rack piled with what appeared to be a great variety of music.

After conducting me into this room and requesting me to make myself at home, my host stepped to the mantel over which was a transmitter something like what I had seen in the office of the Director of Navigation at Corinthus, and pulled out a stop, whereupon in tones sweet and rich, but soft and low the most beautiful orchestral music seemed to float in and fill the room. He then excused himself and withdrew saying that he would rejoin me directly.

I was so charmed with the music that sounded like the far off strains of some grand orchestra, that I made no note of time and was only recalled to my surroundings when Prof. Morris advanced into the room leading a handsome woman of middle age who he introduced to me as his wife. Extending her hand she greeted me most cordially (while the professor shut off the music), welcoming me to her country and particularly to her home. I acknowledged her courtesy in the best language I was able to command and expressed my sincere and heartfelt gratitude for the warm welcome I had received from everyone

---

[4] Bundles of sticks or twigs bound together as fuel.

I had met, especially from herself and generous husband. My hostess was dressed in a house gown, or kind of wrapper, and was certainly a very prepossessing woman. With a most engaging smile, she assured me that in meeting a countryman of her husband's she felt that she was meeting a near relative and with a directness and simplicity that completely captivated me, she expressed the hope that I would reciprocate the feeling. She also insisted—and in this she was joined by her husband, that I should make their house my home all the time and any time that I was in the capital.

As I had had but little time to talk with my host before, the conversation naturally turned to the world we had left and especially to our native country. I briefly outlined the course of events from the time he left the United States down to the present. In all this as may be supposed, he was deeply interested and his charming wife appeared to be not less so. The Civil War was in progress when he left America and it was with great satisfaction he learned that the Union had been preserved and loyal friendship again established between the states. He informed me that he was a young officer in the Navy when the war broke out, but being of southern birth he could not take up arms against his native state and at the same time, he was too loyal to array himself against the federal government. As a way out of it, he resigned and being quite wealthy, he purchased and manned a vessel, and having long cherished a desire for polar exploration, resolved to spend the period during which the war was being waged, in a voyage to the Antarctic regions. Like myself, he had found the passage through the ice barriers and sailed down to the coast of the Iron Republic. As he was familiar with the history of the world and particularly that of the United States down to 1861 when he left it, and as the wonderful country in which I found myself was as new to me as if it had been located on Jupiter of Mars, there was of course far more for me to learn than to tell. But as I knew how great his interest must be in the world he had left more than thirty years before

ch. ends p. 60

and had never heard from since. I forbore asking any questions concerning his adopted country until I had imparted to him as thorough a knowledge as possible of what had taken place in the old world since he left it.

As I warmed up in this endeavor, inspired by the eager interest of both my host and his wife—who listened with rapt attention, I was interrupted by the rustling of a portière[5] behind and, turning, I saw a vision of loveliness that drove the whole subject from my mind and so confused me that as I rose to be introduced, I hesitated and stammered like a schoolboy. There, framed by the arched doorway, with one hand raised to push aside the portière, was a picture to rattle the most stolid and indifferent son of Adam. (You see how naturally I fall back into the American vernacular.) Tall, fair with a wealth of golden brown hair coiled like a turban on the crown of a magnificently poised head, I beheld standing before me the most splendid woman that I had ever gazed upon. Large brown eyes beaming with intelligence, milk white forehead broad and low, a firm mouth, exquisitely chiseled with full ruby lips, a well rounded chin, strong, but relieved by a most charming dimple, perfect teeth and snow white, as I observed when she smiled a most gracious welcome, such was Helen Morris, the daughter of the house, as she appeared to me the first time. I had always been proud of America's beautiful women, of whom I had known many, but never before had I looked upon a woman that so impressed, or I should rather say, overwhelmed me. She was richly attired in the evening dress of that country which heightened the charm of her queenly face and figure. She wore a close-fitting bodice of light blue silk that displayed to perfection the exqui- sitely rounded bust and well-formed waist and extended just high enough to be caught with a pearl shell ornament like an epaulet[6] over the shoulders. Above this was set a rich lace collar

---

[5] A curtain hung over a door or doorway.
[6] An ornamental shoulder piece on an item of clothing.

or yoke of a delicate peach blow tint, which served to empha-size the whiteness of the alabaster throat, close-fitting sleeves of the same stuff revealed, rather than hid, the beautifully molded arms, ending with large ruffles at the wrists. Around the waist was belted a skirt of seal brown velvet extending halfway to the knees and under this was worn a close-fitting knitted garment of dove colored silk that terminated in seal-colored buskins[7] fastened with light blue pearl buttons around the shapely ankle. She looked like a beautiful prima donna[8] before the footlights in full stage costume, every perfection of form and feature was displayed to the greatest possible advantage and as she advanced with natural and unstudied grace. I could not but remark how much more beautiful God's most exquisite creation appeared in this garb than in the starched and stilted skirts as I had been accustomed to seeing them all my life.

She also greeted me cordially and though too polite to appear to notice it, with a sweeping glance she took in my cos-tume and I imagined that I could detect a smile lurking in the corners of her mouth. To a person who had never before seen a man attired in baggy legged trousers that dragged the floor and high glazed collar that cut the chin, I, no doubt, presented quite a ludicrous appearance. As I contrasted myself with her father, gracefully dressed in the old English fashion of knee breeches and ruffles. I could not but perceive that it was to my disadvantage. After the exchange of a few pleasant civilities in which I was as much charmed with the music of her voice as I had been with the beauty of her person, she announced that the evening meal was waiting and taking her father's arm led the way to the dining room leaving me to escort Mrs. Morris, or rather to be escorted by her.

The dining room, or kitchen, for it was all in one, was a cozy room with polished stone floor and at one end was what

[7] Calf-high or knee-high boots.
[8] The principal female singer in an opera or opera company.

ch. ends p. 60

appeared to be a low enameled sideboard, though I found when the meal was served that it was an electric furnace from which the different dishes were taken and set upon the marble-topped table. Everything was served from the dish in which it was cooked and I learned for the first time that culinary operations could be carried on without soot or smoke.

The cooking vessels were set upon paper mats and under each plate was spread a snow white paper napkin while another, neatly folded lay beside it. At the risk of being tiresome I am going thus minutely into these details, my object being to give as clearly as possible an insight into the way these people live. It is with the hope, too, that overworked American women whose lives are one long martyrdom to the washtub, the dishpan, and the ironing table may profit by the simpler and cleanlier customs of a more advanced people. Knowing what American customs were, my host remarked to me that there was enough necessary labor in the Iron Republic to keep everybody employed and so no unnecessary labor was indulged in.

No tablecloths or napkins were laundered, the paper ones used being fully as good and so cheap that the cost was a mere nothing. Even these, after being used were packed in a hamper and exchanged for new ones at half the original cost. They were chemically cleansed and went into pulp again at the factory and so were used over and over.

The professor and his wife sat opposite to each other at the table, which placed me vis-a-vis[9] to the charming daughter. I had been accustomed to social functions of every description and no Beau Brummell was ever more at home at a fashionable dinner party than I.[10] But with this beautiful woman directly in front of me, her radiant face only a few feet from mine and our

---

[9] Face to face.

[10] George Bryan "Beau" Brummell (1778-1840) was an important figure in Regency era of England and, for many years, the arbiter of men's fashion.

knees almost touching under the table, I was as awkward as a country bumpkin at a Lord Mayor's banquet.[11]

They were all kind enough I think, to attribute this to the strangeness of my surroundings and in most gracious ways strove to relieve me of my embarrassment and make me feel at home. During the meal hour, which was a most delightful one, we talked about American customs and then the conversation turned upon American art and literature, in comparison with that of the Iron Republic. In the discussion which followed, I was pitted against the ladies. My host remarking that as he was a citizen of both countries he should be equally proud of the achievements of each. I dilated on our poets, essayists, and novelists and lauded the achievements of our architects and painters; but whether it was the superior numbers of the enemy or superior strategic ability, my native country was made to appear as far behind in these as in the more practical arts of life. The best of the old English writers were not unknown to them, as Prof. Morris carried a well-stocked library in the vessel that bore him to his adopted country. Emerson,[12] Longfellow,[13] Whittier,[14] and many other American writers they were also familiar with as the professor had brought their earlier works to the country and all had been republished and put through many editions. Finally, turning to my host, I said banteringly, "Professor, if your relations to both countries disqualifies you for participating in this discussion or taking sides, it ought to fit you all the better to act as referee between us. You are familiar with what is best in both countries and to your judgment I am

[11] Lord mayor is a title of a mayor of what is usually a major city in a Commonwealth realm, with special recognition bestowed by the sovereign.

[12] Ralph Waldo Emerson (1803–1882) was an American lecturer, philosopher, abolitionist, and poet who led the transcendentalist movement of the mid-19th century.

[13] Henry Wadsworth Longfellow (1807–1882) was an American educator and one of the fireside poets from New England.

[14] John Greenleaf Whittier (1807–1892) was an American Quaker and one of the fireside poets from New England.

ch. ends p. 60

willing to defer: Now, upon the lines we have been debating, which country in your opinion, is entitled to take precedence?"

"This," said the professor after a moment's hesitation, "is a difficult question to answer. To institute a comparison of this kind is like comparing one part of the firmament to the other. Every nation has produced its great men—men who were brilliant in different ways. One part of the firmament has stars as bright as any other part. The human mind has its limitations and probably some men of every race have risen to the limit of human achievement in some things. But while all parts of the firmament may contain bright stars—as bright as the brightest—looking at the sidereal heavens you will observe that one part, taken altogether, is more luminous than another, that is to say has more bright stars. And so, passing judgment on both countries as a whole, I am compelled to say that the Iron Republic has surpassed America or any other nation. America has produced one Longfellow; the Iron Republic many. An essayist like Emerson towers above you like a monarch of the forest; here, they are as the leaves in Vallambrosa's shade.[15] You had one Beecher:[16] here, his name is legion! And so in every field where the human mind has blazed a shining way. I will not say that in America the highway of genius is less exalted, but it is less traveled!"

"But why should that be so," I asked, unwilling to yield the point, "when both nations came from the same parent stock and developed under practically the same climatic conditions?"

"My dear sir," replied the professor with a smile, "that question is easily answered. Admitting the intellectual equality of the two nations, there is every reason why this should excel in every field of human effort except that of bold and cunning acquisitions. The construction of your government and indeed

[15] A reference to the forest of Vallombrosa, known as "shady valley," in the Tuscany region of Italy.

[16] Likely a reference to American theologian and author Edward Beecher D.D. (1803–1895), who was the brother of Harriet Beecher Stowe (1811–1896).

of all the governments of the old world is such as to encourage the prostitution of great talents to selfish personal aggrandizement. The genius which has made your thousands of great politicians and financiers, would have made the same men great, or many of them, with a more unselfish and enduring greatness in this country. Here, Henry Clay[17] or Daniel Webster[18] would never have devoted an hour of time or an iota of talent to the trade of politics; for neither, by taking thought, could have added a cubit to his political stature. The genius that has built up million dollar fortunes in your country, here, would have lain dormant or been more unselfishly applied. What I mean to say is that in this country great talents can only find expression in the fields of art, literature, philosophy, and science, while in your country they may be applied to stock jobbing, financial exploitation, and the trade of politics. All these fields invite talents of the highest order and yield returns more gratifying to our selfish instincts."

"Do I understand that talent counts for nothing here in the race for wealth or political preferment?" I asked with astonishment.

"It counts for little in the race for wealth and absolutely nothing in the race for political preferment," answered my host. "The consequence is that ambition, to be gratified, must be in a measure unselfish and genius must expand and soar in a noble field or remain dormant. You cannot hope to grasp the results of a century of intelligent government building in a few

[17] Henry Clay Sr. (1777–1852) was an American attorney and statesman who represented Kentucky in both the U.S. Senate and House of Representatives. He was the seventh House speaker, the ninth secretary of state, and helped found both the National Republican Party and the Whig Party, and was part of the "Great Triumvirate" of Congressmen, alongside fellow Whig Daniel Webster and John C. Calhoun (1782–1850).

[18] Daniel Webster (1782–1852) was an American statesman who represented New Hampshire and Massachusetts in the U.S. Congress and served as the U.S. Secretary of State under Presidents Harrison, Tyler, and Fillmore. He was also one of the most prominent American lawyers of the 19th century, arguing over 200 cases before the U.S. Supreme Court.

ch. ends next p.

minutes, but you will understand when you have had time for observation," he continued as we left the table.

On our return to the sitting room my host excused himself saying that he had some business affairs to look after which would detain him the better part of the evening. Almost immediately afterward Mrs. Morris also excused herself on the plea of having to look after the affairs of her kitchen, for it appeared that although in affluent circumstances, they kept no servants. This left me alone with the daughter and, for a few moments, we sat in rather an embarrassing silence. The glorious beauty of this woman, her great lustrous brown eyes that seemed to irradiate everything they looked upon, the striking and brilliant costume that revealed so perfectly every charm of her graceful form, made the whole seem to me like a scene in the Arabian Nights,[19] in which I was bewitched and transported from the realm of sober reality into the magical presence of some wonderful princess.

She relieved the situation by rising and asking me if I would not like to hear the news of the day, approaching the contrivance over the mantel from which had issued the music before supper. "You will probably hear a good deal about yourself," she said smiling archly as she proceeded to adjust the bell shaped transmitter.

---

[19] A collection of Middle Eastern folk tales compiled in Arabic during the Islamic Golden Age, also known as *One Thousand and One Nights*.

CHAPTER 7

"Then by all means let us dispense with the news," I pleaded with unfeigned earnestness.

"How would you like to be entertained then?" she asked turning to me. "You can have an opera, lecture, or anything that is going on in the city. Perhaps you would like some music? The National Orchestra plays this evening in the capitol and you can have the full program or any part of it."

"I dearly love music," I replied, "and what I have heard in this country has been remarkably fine; but swelling from mysterious tubes, or bursting from great mechanical contrivances imparts a weirdness to it that serves to heighten the unreality of my present position and surroundings. Do you know," I said with a sincerity that made her burst out laughing, "that I have pinched myself a great many times since I reached these shores in the endeavor to awake? Even now, it would be no surprise to me to start and wake and yawn and open my eyes to find myself back in America and my wonderful experience of the past year a dream."

"I dare say you would be highly gratified to awake at this very moment," she said with just a shade of reproach in her voice.

"Oh no indeed!" I cried with an impetuosity[1] altogether out of keeping with the shortness of our acquaintance, at the same time rising hastily and approaching to where she stood by the mantel. "I would not wake now for worlds. 'If it be,' I said, repeating a fragment from one of her own poets that she had quoted at the table.

"'If it be then that the seeming
Has more of beauty than the real,
If only it be in dreaming
I may find the Land o'Leal
May I not continue dreaming?
Were't not cruel to wake again?
Is not bliss e'en in the seeming
Preferable to real pain?'"

A blush overspread her face, making it even more beautiful than before and I, too, flushed, feeling that I had gone too far for a rank stranger, as it were, from another world.

"Very well," she responded, "I would much dislike to wake you as long as your dream is pleasant; nevertheless," she added with a meaning glance, "I shall reserve the privilege of dashing cold water on you whenever I deem it proper to rouse you to a consciousness of your real position." And turning she walked over to the music stand and began to handle the sheets of music.

This Parthian shot[2] sobered me and I begged her to remember the peculiarity of my situation, being as absolutely cut off from every female acquaintance on earth as if I had landed on another planet. Knowing only her mother and herself and meeting them as the wife and daughter of a countryman, I begged pardon, if like the lonely emigrant who meets a compatriot in a strange land, I presumed too much on a short acquaintance.

---

[1] Impulsively; with sudden emotion.

[2] Parting shot; a cutting gesture or remark delivered while departing. The term is derived from a military tactic made famous by Parthian (Iranian) horse archers, who, at full gallop, would turn their bodies back to shoot at the pursuing enemy.

My words or manner evidently convinced her of my sincerity, for turning and advancing with a world of sympathy in her beautiful eyes, she extended her hand with the most frank cordiality and as I grasped her finger tips, (almost daring to raise them to my lips,) she assured me that her love and admiration for her father made it quite impossible for any countryman of his to be a stranger and begged me to consider her an old friend. The touch of her hand made my blood tingle and the sweet candor of her manner made me feel quite at home again.

"What I was going to remark," I resumed, "was that the mysterious and automatic manner in which this music, news, and other entertaining things you suggest comes to us, heightens the unreality of my surroundings and what I desired to make everything seem more real and less like an illusion, was something to remind me of home and life as I had been accustomed to it. This I presume is a musical instrument," said I, advancing to the piano, "and if you will be kind enough to play something yourself I will enjoy it more than all the orchestra's in the world, over a wire or through a tube."

Without a moment's hesitation she complied and sitting down to the instrument, she played several pieces with great skill and expression. Noticing a number of songs among the music, I asked her if she would sing. She consented, but asked me to waive my objections to the "automatic and mysterious tube," as she preferred a violin obbligato[3] to playing her own accompaniment. Selecting a piece of music, she approached the general utility telephone and pressing a button, asked somebody, somewhere, for the obbligato to the song, giving the title. In a moment, soft and low like the sighing melody of an Aeolian harp,[4] came the prelude to the accompaniment and then in a voice full, round, and sweet, she rendered the

---

[3] Translated from Italian, literally: obligatory. A piece of music performed by a single instrument in accompaniment to a solo part.

[4] Also known as a wind harp; a musical instrument that is played by the wind, named after Aeolus, the ancient Greek god of the wind.

ch. ends p. 75

song, the obbligato swelling and sinking and blending with the rich tones of her cultivated voice as though it were played by a master in the very room where we stood.

Mrs. Morris entered the room while she was singing and when the song was finished, at the request of her daughter, joined with her in a duet, her fine contralto[5] voice blending beautifully with the other's soprano. At its conclusion I was asked for an American song and as a fairly good baritone voice was the one single accomplishment I had been proud of at home, I complied and sang "Rocked in the Cradle of the Deep,"[6] while Miss Morris played an accompaniment. I acquitted myself quite creditably and was gratified when they both admitted that no finer song had been composed in the Iron Republic.

When Mrs. Morris reappeared after dinner, she too, was attired in evening dress made similar to her daughter's, though somewhat plainer, of some pearl grey stuff that was extremely becoming. Upon my risking a cautious compliment on her appearance, the conversation turned on the subject of dress and I soon became aware that woman is woman the world over, be the surroundings what they may. I described to them the latest modes of dress in my country and then there was the inevitable comparison between the different styles of the two countries. When I ventured a rough guess at the number of articles of apparel and adornment one of our fashionable ladies would wear at one time, they threw up their hands in horror and wondered how they had time for anything else but to dress and undress. I expressed my decided preference for the Ironion style as illustrated by their charming costumes, but told them frankly that it would not be tolerated in my country.

---

[5] The lowest female voice or voice part, in range between soprano and tenor, and often shortened to "alto."

[6] Lyrics by Emma Willard (1787-1870) and, based on our research, its earliest composition was in 1840 by one of England's most popular song composers, Joseph Philip Knight (1812-1887).

"And pray what would be the objections to it?" asked my hostess.

"To be perfectly plain with you madam," I replied, "it would be considered too—er—that is, immodest."

"But why?"

"Because, my dear madam, I, it is—that is to say, I am delighted with it myself and can conceive of nothing more becoming," I stammered.

"I am very glad," said Mrs. Morris, but why should this style of dress be considered immodest in your country?

"Because madam, if you will have it," I answered under protest, "it admits of too much exposure of the person."

"Then in the world you came from, one object of woman in dressing is to conceal the beauty of form which nature has bestowed upon them!"

"Yes, madam, that is, it seems so."

"Modest ladies attired as we are, in a drawing room, would blush and be embarrassed?"

"Most undoubtedly madam, at first."

"And yet on the stage where the most beautiful and artistic effects are aimed at, this style of dress is employed?"

"That is true madam. It is also true that at the bathing resorts where the sexes are thrown into the closest juxtaposition, only the rudiments of even the Ironion style are worn."

"Now I will ask you candidly, Mr. Barrington, can you conceive of any more reason why the female form, which artists insist is the most perfect work of creation, should be disguised or concealed, than there is that the symmetrical proportions of a horse should be hidden under skirts, or a beautiful statute covered from the head down with a blanket?"

Smiling at the forceful illustration of my hostess I replied that I could not, though if crooked legged horses and thin shanked, imperfect statutes could influence the fashion, even horses and statues might wear clothes.

"No doubt of it," exclaimed my hostess. "And I seem to

ch. ends p. 75

remember one of good old Aesop's fables about a fox who was unfortunate in the matter of his caudal[7] appendage.[8] May it not be, too," she continued, "that the fashion of conceal-ment owes its origin to sentiments and feelings exactly the reverse of modesty? Is, after all, the revelation of such beauty, as the female figure possesses any more suggestive than its concealment when such beauty is known to exist under the disguise? Indeed," she went on warming up with the subject, "the commissioners excluded a most beautiful statue from one of our parks because of the indecent suggestion of the drapery! Here, we wear three or four garments and combine comfort, beauty, grace, and utility. In your country women wear a dozen or more and the most complimentary thing I can say of them after studying their pictures, is that some are not as ugly as others. I'll dare say if Eve had come forth from the shady bowers of Eden and had met her lord and master dressed in the modern American fashion, the poor man would have scaled the fence and left the garden of his own accord!"

I laughed heartily at this sally,[9] and looking slyly at me, Miss Morris observed that her mother must have some good reason for feeling so strongly on the subject.

"Oh, I make no secret of it," retorted her mother good humoredly. "I was once prevailed on by Professor Morris to array myself in all the glory of the American fashion as it pre-vailed when he left there, and appeared in public full rigged—hoop skirt and all. Ugh! It makes my cheeks burn yet to think of it. Seeing a crowd beginning to follow us. I ran into a house and begged the lady for the love of heaven to hide me while my husband called a carriage. I was taken home in hysterics and literally tearing the flounces and frames from my person, I held them over a flame till the last shred fell into ashes. That is, all but the wire in the hoopskirt; that the professor buried

---

[7] Of or like a tail.

[8] A reference to Aesop's "The Fox Without a Tail."

[9] A witty remark.

and with it the last hope of making an American woman of me! It was weeks before I could muster courage to go on the streets again. Since then my husband has admitted that his preference for American dress only extended to me and that for all other women he thought the style of the country much prettier and more desirable! Ah well, he has gotten over all that now," she concluded, "as you will in time."

I assured her that I was already well over it and in the matter of female dress if nothing else, I was an Iron Republican to the core.

Professor Morris arrived in the midst of a general laugh and remarked pleasantly that it did not appear that I was being ostracized as an alien! He then informed us that he had learned while out that there would be an especial attraction at the capitol that evening in the person of Madame Shafton, who was to sing her latest song, and he had asked an usher from his office to connect us when her turn came. Madame Shafton, I was told, was considered the finest singer in the Republic and a composer of rare merit besides. Indeed, I was informed that in musical circles it was hardly considered good form for a person to play or sing anything except their own compositions. The exceptions being in the case only of music of extraordinary merit.

In the midst of a general conversation some ten minutes afterward a sudden hum of voices penetrated the room from the transmitter and then clearly and distinctly came the words:

> "Ladies and gentlemen I have the honor to bring forward one who is known and honored from one end of the Republic to the other and who has always been a deserved favorite at the capitol."

Then, during the applause which followed, very much in the American fashion, Miss Morris ran to the transmitter and pulling out certain stops, drew what appeared to be a ground

ch. ends p. 75

glass screen before it. At the same time, she turned off the lights leaving us in the dark, except for a pale light, which illuminated the screen from the transmitter. This grew brighter and then I saw like a stereoscopic projection what appeared to be an arena railed off in the pit of a great amphitheater and in this arena an orchestra and in front of it, facing the audience a tall and remarkably fine looking woman. She was dressed in a loose flowing robe in the style of the classical Greek period, with wide sleeves and bound loosely about the waist with a knotted cord. She wore sandals on her feet and a wreath of flowers on her head. The song was rendered and encored, the whole performance being as distinctly audible and visible to us as if we had been in the auditorium.

After it was over and the transmitter had been adjusted to cut off any further proceedings. I asked if the people in the city generally were connected with these places of amusement and was informed that everybody in the city and country was thus connected, who elected to pay for the service.

"If then, anybody may enjoy these entertainments in their homes, where do the audiences come from?" I inquired.

"My dear sir," answered my host, "if it were not for these arrangements it would be impossible to accommodate our people without greatly increasing the number of places of public entertainment. As it is, there is always a certain number who attend, for notwithstanding the perfection off our system of transmission, it is still, more satisfactory to be present in person." I learned on inquiry that this extensive system, which pervaded the entire Republic, was established by the government along with electric lights and railroads. This particular branch of it though, it had been found expedient to let to private individuals in the different cities and communities; the system being let to the bidder guaranteeing the cheapest service. I was also informed that public entertainments of every kind were provided by the government without direct cost to the people, most of the great orators, actors, and musicians being pensioned by the state. "As a result of this," said my host, "poor artists do not afflict the public and good ones are not at the mercy of avaricious managers and irresponsible newspapers." I found afterward that the greater part of these artists were trained in the government conservatories to which they had been sent from the public schools on account of extraordinary talents and aptitude. Those who became really great artists were but on a pension for life, if not forfeited by misconduct. There was no compulsion about it however and those who passed the examinations could renounce their pensions and try their fortunes in a private career, while those who failed to pass could do the barn storming business to the top of their bent.

It occurred to me that real merit might sometimes suffer in the presence of a "pull" as we say here, but my host told me that the veriest barn stormer could have any auditorium in the country on petition of patrons and if he could convince the people that he had merit, they had the power to have him put on the pension list.

"Anyway it must be a terrible drain on the revenues of the government," I ventured to remark.

"On the contrary," replied my host, "less money than the United States squanders on ambassadors and consuls sent to foreign countries to serve the traders and protect the interests of those who have expatriated themselves, provides this great people with the most elevating and instructive diversion that human ingenuity has been able to devise."

It had now grown quite late and, as I was very much fatigued after a day of such remarkable experiences, I was not sorry when Mrs. Morris suggested to her husband that it was long past their usual hour of retiring. My host and family were religious people and we stood with bowed heads while in a few impressive words he returned thanks for the day and invoked the Divine care and protection for the night.

I was conducted to a pleasant room and retired immediately, but though utterly tired out, it was long before I slept. Again and

ch. ends p. 75

again, I asked myself if this could be real and tried to recall a formula I had read somewhere for demonstrating an illusion. The panorama of the day's events, crowned and illumined by the glorious face of Helen Morris, passed before my mind's eye like some old mediaeval picture in which the lustrous face of the Madonna appears irradiating the whole.

Awake or dreaming, I felt that I had met my destiny and that to be, awakened from such a dream would be the crudest prank that fortune could play upon me. And then I went back in imagination to my home in America and tried to recall each event from the beginning of my strange experiences, linking them together and so connecting them down to the present. It could not be an illusion!

And yet as a practical man I could not but admit to myself that it was in some respects remarkably dreamlike. Here I was, a bachelor of twenty-six, who had met some of the most beautiful women in America without having my heart even touched and yet I was already deeply involved with the first and only young women I had met in this wonderland and after an acquaintance of only a few hours!

How long I lay awake I know not, but as exhausted nature began to yield I found myself wondering if there was really such a place as the Iron Republic, or barrier passage, or a ship named the "Wanderer." And then I started violently two or three times as I felt myself precipitated from the flying train on which I had ridden that day, or imagined that I was falling from a runaway aeroplane miles and miles above the earth!

When I awoke the next morning, it was with the sound of music in my ears and the first rays of the rising sun shining in at my window. As I listened to the all-pervading harmony that seemed to swell out over the landscape in every direction, I opined from the grand and stately measure that it was a kind of hymn or anthem, evidently played on some great mechanical instrument at a high elevation. I arose and went to my window but I could by no means make out from what direction the sweet sounds came. Though I had retired quite late the night before and it was earlier than I was in the habit of rising, I felt very much refreshed. I could perceive from the invigorating and bracing air that the capital must be located on a high plateau, for the atmosphere had all the crispness of mountain air. The view from my window was different from what I had ever seen in any city before. Instead of a dreary waste of housetops ornamented with clothes horses[10] and chimney flues, as far as the eye could reach I saw pretty cottages of brick and stone surrounded by spacious gardens and grounds. As I looked over these highly cultivated tracts, I thought of what I had read of ancient Babylon, that enough provisions could be raised within its walls with what was stored to withstand a siege of twenty years. The music, which had awakened me continued for some five minutes and then ceased and died away in the distance like the musical cadence of a deep toned bell. Dressing I went down into the sitting room and finding no one there walked out on the veranda. My friend's house stood in the midst of quite extensive grounds, which with the exception of the flower garden about the house, was set in vines and fruit trees. As I looked down through a labyrinth of green, I caught the glimpse of a scarlet figure and though I could but see the flashes of color through the intervening foliage, something in the free and graceful movement told me that it was the daughter of the house.

With my heart beating as it never did at the sight of any woman before, I descended from the veranda and picking my way through the dew-laden grass, I approached her. She did not see me as her face was turned the other way and I had the opportunity of admiring her beautiful form in another garb and with different surroundings. She wore a knitted scarlet jersey that fitted perfectly and was belted about the waist with a hempen[11] girdle. Below the girdle, it broadened into a skirt that fell gracefully to the tops of the waterproof boots of oiled canvas

---

[10] Frame on which washed clothes are hung to air dry.
[11] Made of hemp.

ch. ends p. 75

that buttoned quite up to the knees. The tight fitting sleeves covered her wrists and the turned up collar completely hid her white neck and throat. Her hair fell in tresses to her waist and but for the jaunty straw hat that surmounted the whole, she would have been almost a facsimile of an American Indian maiden as they are pictured in the old school books. She was picking grapes and as I came up, she turned and greeted me with a smile. I had wondered when I came out, if she would appear as enchanting under the severer ordeal of daylight and sunshine as she had the night before, and the first glance showed her to be even more so. Her cheeks were as rosy as a sun-kissed peach and her deep brown eyes seemed to have caught an opaline[12] tint from the morning sky. Although she looked so charmingly fresh and beautiful that had I dared I would probably have made a fool of myself. As I feasted my eyes on the fresh loveliness of her face, she blushed slightly and looked down into the basket she carried on her arm.

"You are an early riser," I said taking the basket from her and pulling down the vine from which she had been picking grapes.

"It is our custom to rise with the sun," she replied. "I am glad to find that you did not wake up in America this morning."

"If I had," I said looking into her face so ardently that her eyes fell before mine. "I should have been the most miserable man in that country."

"Did you wake in time to hear the matin?"[13] she asked lightly as if to give another turn to the conversation.

"Do you mean that grand music that seemed to pervade everything?"

"Yes, that is the matin and is played every morning at sunrise. Did you like the music?"

"Indeed I thought it was magnificent."

"Oh, thank you," she said with a gratified smile; it was by a very dear friend of mine and I am so glad you liked it."

---

[12] Opalescent.
[13] A term relating to daybreak or the early a.m.

"Indeed," I exclaimed, "and who is this accomplished friend?"

"Professor Hallam of the National Conservatory." Those few words robbed the sun of half its brightness and the world of half its charm to me. Even the grape that I had put into my mouth seemed to lose its sweetness. After all, this brilliant creature had a very dear friend and what interest could she possibly take in me further than to indulge a generous sympathy for a wandering and lost man without a people and without a country.

"Does he play this hymn every morning?" I asked.

"Oh, no indeed! As a rule he improvises a new piece every morning and never plays the same one two days in succession, unless there are special requests for it to be repeated."

"He must be a wonderful man," I remarked, "to improvise such wonderful music, but it is more wonderful still, that he should be able to repeat such improvisations afterward."

"He doesn't do that," she answered. "Everything that is played on the Grand Harmonium, is by a mechanical device, registered, that is, a copy of the music is made and can be preserved."

"And is this matin as you call it a public function?" I inquired.

"Entirely so," was the reply. "It was instituted by Professor Hallam when he was called to the head of the Conservatory. It was his idea and these Matins and Nocturns are his 'fad,' if I may employ an American term I heard you use last night, but a most beautiful one nevertheless."

"Where does this music come from?" I asked looking around for its probable source, "and how far can it be heard?"

"It is played from the dome of the Conservatory and can be heard for many miles around, when the weather is favorable," she answered. In reply to my further question if it was a function that was performed in all parts of the Republic, I was informed that it was a purely local affair originating with Professor Hallam, but that quite a number of cities and communities had adopted it and it was obtaining great favor with the people.

ch. ends next p.

"From his position and ability, this Professor Hallam must be—er, that is, quite an old man," I ventured blunderingly.

"I would judge him to be about your age," she answered with an arch smile. "I do not know how you reckon your age in America, but it is not considered distressingly old in this country."

My heart turned to lead as she went on to speak of his great genius, his wonderful compositions and his national fame; it sank like the mercury in a Dakota blizzard. She told me with an evident glow of pride, that he had taken a special interest in her, and that she was indebted to him for what little knowledge of music she possessed.

I heard all this with pretty much the same feelings that the condemned man hears the judge, in long drawn judicial platitudes, depict the enormity of his crime. It was plainly to be seen that she greatly admired this musical prodigy, if nothing more. Noticing my downcast look, she rallied me by asking what I thought of her working dress. I felt like telling her that Mother Eve's dress of fig leaves would be gorgeous, if only she wore it, but simply remarked that I thought it very pretty and convenient. She told me that this style of dress was worn by the women and girls generally, for walking and outdoor work.

A call from Mrs. Morris interrupted us, and saying that her mother wanted the grapes for breakfast, my companion led the way to the house. Arriving there, she took the basket and telling me that I would probably find her father in the library, she passed into the kitchen through the back door.

On entering, I was warmly greeted by my host and in a few minutes breakfast was announced. The meal was simple but most excellent, consisting chiefly of cereals, with butter, milk, and fruit. Coffee was also served. After a short invocation by the head of the house, we took our places at the table in the same order as the evening before and without the slightest pretense at formality or ceremony, the breakfast was served. After a few minutes conversation, mostly referring to my impressions of my surroundings, Professor Morris remarked that it was their custom, in lieu of conversation, to take the "current news" during the meal hour, especially at breakfast. He was a very busy man, he said, and tried to dispose of the day so as to get the most out of it. Then at the request of her father, Miss Helen rose and going back into the front room manipulated the telephone in some way and returned to the table. Almost immediately, a voice began to speak, apparently from overhead, and looking up I noticed another transmitter in the center of the ceiling similar to the one in the front room.

Clear and distinct came the words, as if a good reader was reading from the columns of a newspaper. "Ironia, 7 o'clock. Morning resume." And then followed general news reports from every part of the Republic, agricultural and government reports, local news items, and in general the matter which goes to make up the news pages of our daily papers. There was a condensed account of the voyage of the "Wanderer," from an interview with Captain Brent, and an item stating that I was the guest of Prof. Morris of the Naval College. We lingered at the table some minutes after the meal was concluded to get the sum of this "resume" and it still continued after we left the room. We had gotten all of the current news though, and my host could not spare the time to take the literary review, which followed. For an hour or two more, I was informed this "resume" would continue, giving out reviews, essays, poetry, fiction, humor, and purely literary matter of every description, which the ladies enjoyed at their morning work.

CHAPTER 8

When we left the ladies and passed into the library, my host informed me that he was at my service for the day and would take pleasure in showing me about the city, which besides being the capital, was one of the most beautiful in the Republic. "I have ordered a carriage which will be here in a few minutes," he said, "and we will, if you please, devote the forenoon to an inspection of our principal public buildings. This afternoon we can take a general view of the city. And now," he continued, "if you will consent to wear a suit of my clothes until you can have a tailor supply you, I think it will save you some annoyance. The unusual style of your dress must attract attention and it is not pleasant to be the center of interest for the curious crowd."

I thanked him and availing myself of his kind offer, went up to my room and made the change. As we were of about the same size and proportions, the clothes fitted me admirably, and though I felt at first like a baseball player or Richelieu[1] at a masquerade, I was far more comfortable than I would have been in my own outlandish garb. Taking our places in a kind of motor

[1] Likely a reference to Armand Jean du Plessis, Duke of Richelieu (1585–1642), known as Cardinal Richelieu, who was a French clergyman and statesman — and the primary antagonist of the 1844 historical novel *The Three Musketeers* by French author Alexandre Dumas (1802–1870).

carriage or landau[2] that had arrived, we were whirled rapidly through many beautiful streets and squares to the capitol. This magnificent building of which I have a number of photographs on board of my vessel, is modeled after the Roman Pantheon but much larger. Also instead of one, there are four columned entrances of white and blue marble, that rose to the height of the dome and then from a richly ornamented fringe broke away into moorish towers of great beauty. Each of these entrances was a building of itself and above the pillared rotunda which forms an entrance to the auditorium under the great dome, are several stories divided into offices for the different departments of the government. From the second floor, each of these opened into a passageway on a great gallery that ran entirely around the auditorium and thus they were connected above the ground and within the building. Passing into one of these great vestibules, we ascended a broad stairway on one side of the gallery, from which my friend said a better view could be had of the great auditorium. There were elevators on the other side, but as we were only going up to the first floor, we took the stairs.

Any adequate description of this magnificent place as it appeared to me when we walked out on the broad gallery is beyond my powers. The auditorium, I was informed, is two hundred feet in diameter beneath the dome, making the circuit of the gallery on which we stood about six hundred feet. This balcony was supported all around on graceful columns and surmounted by a heavy bronze balustrade,[3] which is a rare work of art. On the floor of this immense amphitheater, was a platform or arena, some fifty feet in diameter, enclosed with a railing and furnished with chairs and desks for the use of the members of the National Assembly. These were rolled to the back of the platform as the place had been used for a concert the night before and I immediately recognized it as the place

---

[2] A four-wheel covered carriage with front and back passenger seats and a roof divided into two parts that can be lowered or detached.

[3] An ornamental railing at the side of a staircase, balcony, or terrace.

I had seen in miniature. From this platform, the seats in the auditorium extended back to and under the broad gallery that ran around the walls making, with the balcony, the professor informed me, a seating capacity for about fifteen thousand persons. The seats in the body of the auditorium were built of marble with numerous aisles leading down, while those on the balcony were of bronze.

Around the entire amphitheater, where the great dome sprang from the supporting walls, was a heavy gilded cornice supported by ornate capitals resting on pillars in bas-relief[4] that extended to the floor of the balcony. Between this cornice and a heavy gild mold a few feet under it was the National picture gallery, where displayed were portraits of presidents and notables of the Republic in every field of effort. Only a small part of this space had been consumed and I was informed that if the present high grade of eligibility was maintained, it would require at least a thousand years to fill this gallery. I was assured that to get one's portrait in this place was a greater distinction than it was to have been crowned victor in the ancient Olympian Games, or to be buried in Westminster Abbey.[5]

Above the cornice, was undoubtedly the most magnificent and artistic frieze[6] ever created by the hand of man. Over a ground work of rolling cloud masses, black and storm driven, that was piled around the circle of this grand cornice like a horizon, were pictures representing in allegory the history of the nation. Even if I were capable, the poverty of our language forbids an adequate description of this amazing work of art. The first picture was a ship leaving an old world city with all the attendant scenes that could portray the emotions of friends and kindred in the act of parting. The next was the same ship, lone

[4] A method of molding, carving, or stamping in which the design stands out from the surface but no part is completely detached from it.

[5] A historic, mainly Gothic church in the City of Westminster, London, England, and, since Edward the Confessor (c. 1003–1066), a burial site for English and British monarchs.

[6] A broad horizontal band of sculpted or painted decoration.

ch. ends p. 93

and wave beaten, fighting its way through the icebergs of a polar sea. In the next, the voyagers are landing with thanksgiving on a newfound land. And so it went on, the wonderful pictures all trending in the same direction with the storm driven clouds and illustrating pioneer life, agriculture, art, science, religion, and war and making an historical panorama which it would require days and even weeks to properly study and appreciate.

"And have you had wars in this country?" I asked as my eye rested on a most realistic scene of fire and carnage.

"The most cruel and horrible perhaps of any nation in modern times," answered my friend. "That was before my arrival in the country, but the very ground on which this building stands has been soaked in human blood and piled with the mangled bodies of the slain. The present order, so far removed from even the contingency of war, was by no means a bloodless achievement as you will find when you have time to read the history of the country."

Above the frieze which I have been trying to describe, was a beautiful and artistic border of angels flying swiftly in the direction indicated by the development of the allegorical procession below. From this to the zenith, the great sky-blue dome was relieved with dashes of flecks of cloud in representation of the firmament, with here and there an airy picture from the ancient mythology. It was lighted by many windows, but they were covered with glass so exactly tinted to match the surface in which they were set that they were scarcely distinguishable. The whole interior surface was set with electric jets, which by night appeared like stars shining in the sky. This was the chamber of deputies and though the National Assembly was not in session, it was open, as indeed, I was informed that it stood open to the public always, night and day and was one of the attractions of the capitol to visitors. Quite a number of people, evidently strangers, were scattered about the auditorium, singly or in groups, admiring and descanting[7] on the beauties of the place. I noticed, too, several ladies and gentlemen, apparently art students, who had their easels set at different places on the balcony and were engaged in copying pictures from the frieze.

Standing within the railing of the platform, a janitor was demonstrating by some experiments the remarkable acoustic qualities of the place. Tapping a desk with a gavel, which sounded in the gallery like the report of a six-pounder, he requested us all to stand still for a moment and then he snapped his fingers and the sound came to the furtherest gallery as distinctly as the crack of a whip. Next, he whispered a sentence, which was perfectly audible, and then he took up a pen and wrote a line on a sheet of paper lying on a desk. The scratching of the pen could be heard to the remotest seat more than a hundred feet away.

I remarked to my guide that the debates here must be of a very exciting character to require so large an auditorium, especially as every word spoken here could be heard by the people in their homes. In reply, he told me that they were exciting sometimes, but the most interesting events and those that drew the largest audiences were when distinguished men of national reputation came to claim "privilege." To make me understand this, he explained that any person, man or woman, at the request of the deputy from their province, by recommendation of their Commonwealth Assembly or on a petition signed by one thousand citizens, could claim the privilege of this floor to speak on any measure of public policy, the same as if he were a national senator. On occasions when men of great fame came here to discuss questions of importance, the vast auditorium was filled to its utmost capacity. Also at the inauguration of presidents, the people came in great numbers from all parts of the country. As a matter of fact I was told that

---

[7] Talking or commenting at length; discourse.

ch. ends p. 93

during the sessions there was always people enough to make a large audience.

After taking in the auditorium we passed into other parts of the great building where were the different departments of the government. We went through the departments of Justice, Agriculture, Transportation and Public Utilities, Subsistence, Finance, and Progression. The last was really a department of internal improvement, corresponding somewhat to our department of the interior. There was no departments of state, war, or navy. The Post Office Department was one of the largest and was in a separate building, as the postal system there includes a species of banking and express.

After going through the capitol, we inspected several other fine public buildings situated in the Capitol Square, a large park-like area which was laid off with trees, shrubs, and flowers and adorned with fountains and statuary. In a paved court facing the main entrance to the capitol was a circular monument or pillar of solid iron, thirty feet high and ten or twelve feet in diameter on which stood a colossal bronze statue of what was apparently a working man with a sledge hammer thrown back in the attitude of striking a blow. A bronze scroll on the face of the pillar was inscribed with the words, "The state was made for man, and not man for the state." The statue, the professor told me, was of a blacksmith named Adam Holt, who was the real founder of the Republic, and the pillar was cast entirely of the cannon, which had been used in the Great War that preceded its establishment. Every president who was inaugurated took the oath of office, I was told, with his hand on the pillar, and his first official utterance was to declare in the hearing of the people, the words of the scroll.

We went through the National Conservatory of Music, The Historical Museum, The Marine College (of which my host was the head), and the National College of Experimental Sciences. Everywhere my companion was received with the greatest courtesy and seemed to be held in the highest esteem.

I entered the conservatory with an interest enhanced by what I had heard of its talented president and recognized him at once from having seen him on the stage at Corinthus. My first glance, when I was introduced to him showed me that I was in the presence of that sporadic production of nature that we call genius. He was a young man but prematurely bald and a decided stoop made him appear short, though he was really of medium height. A fringe of light brown hair clustered around his large head and his complexion was as fair as that of Helen Morris. His eyes were blue and rather watery and impressed me, even when he was speaking to me, with the idea that he was listening to something afar off. Apparently he had never shaved, for the scant brown beard, that grew upon his face was as fine as a woman's hair. When I expressed my high appreciation of his musical production of that morning and told him how his accomplishments had been lauded by his fair pupil, he smiled in a pleased way and remarked that Miss Morris was, herself, the possessor of fine musical talents. He then launched into a dissertation on the divine art and I saw by the futile attempts of Prof. Morris to ring him off and turn the conversation into other channels that he was "wound up" on that subject. He dilated on Miss Morris' great capacity for harmony and deplored her fatal deficiency in technique, in such a way as to show that he had thoroughly analyzed her from the musical standpoint. I knew nothing of his musical terms but was an interested listener while he talked about his beautiful pupil and encouraged him to the top of his bent, although I could but smile as I noticed that he discussed her exactly as he would a piano or violin. I wanted to "size him up" as we say in America and tried him on other subjects, but outside of his art, he was as blank as the backside of a tombstone. I asked him about the manner of his inspiration and he told me that he caught strains from the wind in the trees, from the singing of birds, from everything he heard that was not discordant. He informed me that he had a light Aeolian harp attached to his aeroplane and as he sailed

ch. ends p. 93

through the air he had only to arrange the music it made for him to get his very best compositions. We went up into the "tower of music" and he described to us the perfections of his great instrument with as much pride and enthusiasm as an American would talk about his first baby. From a musical standpoint, he was decidedly interesting.

After walking over the beautiful grounds, we returned to the Marine building, where in the private office of my host, we remained until the hour for lunch.

"There is so much to tell you," he replied to a question of mine in regard to the government, "that I hardly know how to begin. Take the elective franchise now; we have no voting for officers here as you do in the United States. Every man here, who is a citizen, has the same chance to hold office and that is unquestionably the only truly representative form of government."

"Do you call that a truly representative system," I asked, "which gives the most stupid and untalented man an equal opportunity for office and political preferment that the brilliant, the forceful and the laborious enjoy?"

"That is just why I do call it truly representative," answered the professor. "The great masses of mankind are stupid and untalented; without disparaging your country, which is also mine, I may safely say that ninety-nine out of every hundred men are untalented plodders. And yet, except in accidental cases, mediocre men never have a seat in your national legislature unless they have inherited or in some other way obtained money enough to buy it. The representation is almost wholly by the brilliant or forceful men; men who can by strength, genius, or cunning control circumstances and compel fortune. In the Iron Republic, every class of men—the brilliant, the forceful, the untalented and stupid—may hope to enjoy the honors of office in the proportion that they exist."

"I am curious to know by what means you secure this average of representations," said I, "for certainly in politics.

I can conceive of no method which will not give the race to the swift and the battle to the strong."

"Well, to begin with," answered my friend, "we have no such thing here as politics, in the sense that the word is used in the United States. There, if there has been no improvement since I left the country, politics simply means that fierce, desperate, and continuous struggle which goes on between brainy, unscrupulous, and self-seeking men for place and power, where the strongest and most conscienceless stand to win and where success means selfish aggrandizement and gain. It is destructive to the finest sentiments of manhood and has debauched and prostituted the noblest intellects."

"But you must admit," I insisted, "that the strong and brainy men are best fitted to devise laws for the government, not only of themselves, but also of the stupid and untalented—if we may continue to so designate the ninety and nine plodders."

"I admit nothing of the kind," retorted the professor. "On the contrary, I believe that even in America, the least talented lawmakers are the most useful, because they have less reason to be influenced by considerations of personal ambition. It is with great intellect now, as it was with great skill and strength in the olden time; it is almost invariably used to advance the interests of its possessor at the expense of the less gifted. I will agree that the more capable a man is, integrity and other sterling qualities being equal, the better fitted he is to devise laws for his fellows, provided his own selfish interests are in no way involved, and that is just the condition here. The laws for the government of this Republic are devised by its scientists, scholars and philosophers, men who for the most part have no offices and no power to obtain them. Their efforts being thus absolutely untrammeled by considerations of selfish interest or ambition, are necessarily unselfish and for the good of their kind. Here, laws are originated by the people and adopted by them, the function of their representatives being simply to

ch. ends p. 93

properly frame and execute statutes at their command. In other words, they are the servants and not the masters of the people."

"But," said I with a trace of impatience which I could not conceal, "you surely cannot expect that men who are capable of devising wise measures of public policy will do so without the hope of reward, either in the way of gain or gratified ambition!"

"Indeed I do expect it," said my friend, "no man who ever had great thoughts could keep them to himself even though publishing them brought him persecution instead of profit. The finest intellects of the world have delved in the domains of science, philosophy, and religion without gain and why not in that noblest field for genius, the art of human government?"

"Well," said I laughing, "we have a saying in America, that 'you can't argue against success,' and in the presence of the monumental success of the ages I am without an argument. But I am curious to understand how it is done."

"Nothing in the way of human government is so simple," replied my friend, "unless it be an absolute despotism.[8] We start with the assumption that any man or unmarried woman with the necessary qualifications of age, character, and education is entitled to be a citizen. Accordingly when he or she goes to the proper authorities with a certificate from the register or supervisor of their primary that they are twenty years old and that they are under conviction of no crime, with a diploma from the public school, they have issued to them a seal like this (drawing from his purse the medal I had seen him use at the sub-treasury in Corinthus), which invests them with all the rights and privileges of full citizenship in this Republic, or to speak technically, they are 'franklins' of the first grade. Every office under the government is now as accessible to the dullest of these franklins as to the brightest. To make you understand more perfectly, it is necessary to explain to you the political divisions of the country. First, we have the 'primary.'

---

[8] A country or political system where the ruler holds absolute power; tyranny.

This consists, technically, of an area seven miles square, or forty-nine square miles and containing one thousand franklins. In practice, though, the extent of the primary is purely arbitrary, depending upon the quality of the soil, natural resources of the section and consequent density of population, and may contain one thousand franklins or any fraction thereof over three hundred. Of course, citizens can live in unorganized territory, that is, where no primary has been constituted; but this deprives them to some extent of their privileges if they are franklins of the first grade, as they have no opportunity to vote their seal and so pass into the second grade. If they are franklins of the second grade though, they can vote their seal for the third grade in any primary in the commonwealth in which they live. Any citizen, too, can exercise the 'appellate' franchise and vote on the acceptance or rejection of laws in the primary most convenient to him. These primaries correspond to your precincts in America, and in the center or part most accessible to all, is the shire, where is located the post office, sub-treasury, and public school. The only elective officer in the primary is the supervisor (the lowest civil officer under the state), who after one year's service becomes, by virtue thereof, primary magistrate. On the first of December the franklins meet at their shire and this officer is chosen by lot, every citizen having an equal chance. On the first of January, the lucky man on whom the choice has fallen assumes the duties of the office, his predecessor becoming magistrate in place of the retiring incumbent. A primary magistrate exercises the functions of notary public and trial justice, has control of post office, public school, and sub-treasury, and represents his primary in the commonwealth council, a body corresponding very nearly to your board of county commissioners. He employs postmasters, bookkeepers, schoolteachers, and all who work for the state in his primary at prices fixed by law. It is the principle of despotism—the simplest and most economical form of government—applied

ch. ends p. 93

by the people themselves. 'Vox despoto, vox populi.'[9] The supervisor is simply a subordinate officer or assistant to the magistrate with the power to act in his place when required."

"After a citizen has served successfully as a supervisor and magistrate, he becomes a franklin of the second grade and is eligible to the next higher office under the state, which is that of commonwealth deputy in the provincial assembly. This body corresponds to your state legislature. One week after the primary election, the commonwealth election is held, which is participated in by all ex-magistrates in the commonwealth, and one is chosen commonwealth representative in the provincial assembly. The choice for all civil officers is by lot. A week later, the provincial elections are held and from the body of ex-commonwealth deputies one is chosen to represent the province in the national senate. All of the newly elected bodies meet on the first day of January and organize and the new senate from the whole number of ex-senators in the Republic choose a new president. The primary elections occur annually, the commonwealth elections biennially and the provincial and presidential elections quadrennially, the terms of office being respectively, one, two, and four years. A citizen is, by virtue of his seal, a citizen of the first grade; after he has served as magistrate, he is in the second grade. After serving as deputy in the provincial assembly, he is a franklin of the third grade, and when he has been elected national senator he advances to the fourth grade. After he has served as president, he has no grade at all, having no longer the right to vote or participate in any election. No citizen is eligible to the same office more than once and, after serving in any of the capacities mentioned, becomes eligible to the next office above and holds that grade if he does not go higher until he reaches the age limit, which is sixty years for the first grade and seventy for the others.

"As with the exercise of the franchise in America, some of our

---

[9] Translated from Latin: The voice of absolute power is the voice of the people.

citizens never contest for any office, having no desire for public life and it being entirely optional with them. When a man is out of office, he is only a private citizen having no advantage over any other franklin in the Republic, except merely his eligibility, in common with all others of his grade, to the office next above the one he has held. Retiring presidents are an exception, as by virtue of having held every office under the state, they are considered preeminently qualified and become life members of the supreme cabinet, which body is composed of ex-presidents and three citizens of the first grade, chosen for distinguished ability and appointed by the incoming president with the approval of the senate. This supreme cabinet serves as an advisory council to the president and as a national board of arbitration, to which is referred all vexed questions of internal administration. It is the highest authority in the Republic and by its sanction; the president has the right to veto. Can you conceive of any scheme of government simpler than this?" asked my friend. "Our financial, judicial and penal systems are just as simple and satisfactory, but we have not time to go into them now."

"The scheme certainly possesses the merit of simplicity." I replied, "and yet under it, is it not possible, probable—aye, extremely probable, that a controlling majority in these legislative bodies may be wholly incapable of framing suitable laws for a great state? My observation has been that men are egotistical and obstinate in the proportion that they are incompetent, and a majority of such men, it seems to me, would not only fail to legislate wisely, but would prevent a capable minority from doing so."

"My dear sir," exclaimed the professor, "you have not yet grasped the first principles of legislation in this great country. It is not the exclusive function of any of these legislative bodies to originate legislation. They may, indeed, devise and propose laws, but they have no power to enact any whatever for the government of the people. Here is where the elective franchise comes in, as every law, whether proposed by the National

ch. ends p. 93

Senate for the Republic, the provincial assembly for the province, or the commonwealth council for the local government of the primaries must be referred to the people and its acceptance or rejection determined by their vote. Wise measures of public policy are originated, for the most part, by scholars and publicists and when they are elaborated and perfected by public discussion, they are properly framed and submitted to the people in the appellate elections. It is the appeal to the people for an expression of their will on the subject. The people may take the initiative and compel legislative bodies to propose laws. This is a prerogative though, that is never exercised, for legislators knowing the alternative are always willing to propose any legislation demanded by their constituents. You want to bear in mind that there are no political parties here such as you have in America, consequently there is not the vindictive strife and party feeling that you have there. There are no questions of personal ambition or party expediency to be considered and no motive to swerve any legislator from the most absolutely unselfish efforts for the public weal."[10]

"There must certainly be differences of opinion on measures of public policy." I suggested.

"There are differences of opinion, of course, on nearly all measures that are proposed and they are discussed by the press and the people and then settled by vote of the sovereign citizens. But as there is no necessary connection between the success of these measures and that of any individual in the nation, the discussions are always moderate and intelligent. Unmarried women of legal age and widows with the necessary qualifications are franklins of the first grade and share with men the appellate franchise."

"Pray what compensation do these different legislative officers receive?" I asked.

"Primary supervisors and magistrates receive one and two

---

[10] For the welfare of the community; the general good.

dollars a day respectively, the year round because they are constantly employed," answered the professor. "Provincial deputies receive three dollars a day for the time they are in session, national senators receive four dollars, and presidents get five dollars for their full time as do members of the supreme cabinet, for they are constantly employed. There is no mileage, as the railroads are owned by the state and it costs them nothing to travel."

"Five dollars a day for the president of a great nation!" The statement fairly took my breath.

"That is very munificent[11] pay," said my friend, "but as they give up all other business as well as their homes, and have to reside at the capitol, it is not considered too much, though their labor is intrinsically worth no more than that of the man who lays brick or shovels dirt."

"This is indeed a remarkable government!" I exclaimed.

"My fellow countryman," said the professor rising, "I have the kindest memories of your country, for it is the land of my birth. But you have a very imperfect system of government. It is by no means representative and admits of more corruption than could exist under an intelligent despotism. It has been so with all previous attempts at popular government. It is an elastic system and heretofore with boundless territory and immense unused resources, it has been adequate. Congestion in the state as in the human body is fatal and you will ultimately reach a period of congestion. The great billows in mid-ocean roll grandly on without danger and without noise, save a deep soothing murmur. It is only when they reach their outmost bounds and dash themselves on the rock-bound coast to be thrown back in broken, foaming masses, that the angry roar of the breakers is heard, sending terror to the heart of the mariner. As long as you have unoccupied territory for your increasing tides of population to flow out upon, your people

---

[11] Very generous.

ch. ends next p.

will have homes and as long as the majority of them have homes and property, you are safe, for it is the illusion of all partially civilized people that the object and end of government is to protect property. But under your system, the time will come when comparatively few people will own most of the property and control the means of subsistence: then, they will logically combine for mutual protection and aggression and learning the terrible power of combination, will inevitably throttle the spirit of liberty and crush the life blood out of your people. On the other hand, a few men in whom the love for wealth and power has extinguished the love of liberty and their fellow men, owning all the wealth and by the power of that wealth controlling production, transportation, legislation, everything! On the other hand, millions of people only a few generations removed from the noblest and most heroic ancestors reduced to the conditions of serfs! Aye, to even a worse condition, for the medieval serf might work and fight for his master, but with your hundred-handed machinery to produce and the blind greed which will deprive the masses of the power to consume, their services will be dispensed with. Their labor will not be required and there is nothing their masters will want them to fight for as they will possess everything. There is the picture for you, sir: heartless greed, oppression, ill-gotten wealth fortified by legislation and protected by hired minions on one side, and on the other, millions who cry for the opportunity to earn bread! And if you want it shaded, there is dynamite and gunpowder and gorgeous combustible villas, all great smoke makers!"

My companion had been pacing the floor excitedly as he poured out these burning words, but now stopping before me his mood suddenly changed and he smiled broadly.

"Why bless me. I am talking to you as though your destiny was bound up in the United States and you were going back there next week, when as a matter of fact we are, both of us, absolutely cut off and that country is no more to us than the lost Atlantis or the cities of the plain! Come, I don't know how you feel, but this great outflow of words seems to have left a void that reminds me that it is about the hour for lunch."

Stepping to the ubiquitous transmitter he gave some orders about a carriage and I heard him say something about a two seater at the hour of fourteen.

Passing out of the building we walked through the handsome grounds of Capitol Square and had barely reached the Boulevard that surrounded it when a light carriage came whizzing down upon us, in which we took our seats and were propelled swiftly to my friend's house in the suburbs.

CHAPTER 9

"I have been greatly interested in what you have told me about your government." I said as we rode along, "but one thing you did not explain I would like to know, and that is how the lots are cast which elects one man to office out of the great number of candidates."

"Now," said my friend, "by a fortunate circumstance, you can have an opportunity of seeing just how it is done, as a magistrate has recently resigned in one of the commonwealths of this province to accept a position in the sub-treasury at Aegia in the province of Vandalia and if you remember, there was an item in the news current this morning which stated that an election would be held tomorrow to fill the vacancy occasioned by the supervisor taking his place. It is only about an hour's run on the Ironia and Olympian railway and you can go down and see it for yourself which will be better than any description you could have of it."

It was accordingly arranged that I should run down the next morning and take it in.

When we arrived at the house of my friend, I found a gentleman waiting for me with a tape line and a book of cloth samples who was introduced as a very capable furnisher. I learned that my host had asked him to call and take my measure for an outfit. I went up to my room with the outfitter and was surprised at the excellent quality of his samples, there being no shoddy or inferior goods in the lot. I intimated to him that as I had a very complete wardrobe and as the period of my sojourn in that country was uncertain, I did not desire anything expensive, preferring something, rather, of good appearance without regard to durability. The smiling tailor told me though, that he had no goods that would not wear for years, all being equally well made and the only difference being in the weight of the material. Inspecting a piece of black cashmere, I asked him if he could guarantee the dye to retain the luster and to my astonishment was informed that he did not handle any dyed cloths at all, everything he had being in the natural color of the wool, which included every shade of handsome suitings of the finest and firmest texture. Remarking the excellence of the quality, I volunteered the compliment that his factories evidently turned out better goods than ours, whereupon he informed me that every piece was woven by hand and that there was not a cloth factory in the Republic! In the meantime, I had made my selection and he was engaged in taking my measure.

"Do you mean to tell me," I asked with astonishment, "that a nation so far advanced as yours does not use machinery in the manufacture of cloth?"

"None at all," was the reply. "They used to, long before my time, but under the Republic no factories are allowed."

"And do you weave this cloth, or do you have to go around and find it among the private individuals who weave it?" I asked.

"Oh, I simply go to the Government Exchange, which takes it from the weavers, and get what I want."

"Does the government speculate in this cloth or simply store it and sell it for the weavers?"

"The government does not speculate on anything," replied the outfitter. "It takes this cloth, giving the weaver in exchange, the price established by the Bureau of Subsistence, which is based on the weight and weave of the goods. It is then sold to whoever wants it at a slight advance which is the seigniorage,[1] or principal source of revenue for the support of the state."

"Then there is no competition," I remarked. "I suppose the prices for the different grades are purely arbitrary with this bureau."

"No, the price of nothing is arbitrary," returned the tailor. "The value of everything being fixed by the average cost of production, as ascertained by the bureau in the most careful and scientific manner."

"There must be," said I, "some unsaleable goods made, as there is in my country: does the exchange have to take them at the production price, regardless of what they will sell for."

"The exchange sometimes has goods that will not sell for the established price by reason of their undesirability, damage in storage, or other causes. When that is the case, they are cut to the selling point. It frequently happens too, especially with agricultural productions, that the price of one article is reduced, while that of other things, which compete with it or displace it, is raised. The bureau has all of that in hand and the business is reduced to a science. The exchange also has the right to reject anything and so producers keep in touch with it and thus know what the public demand is for."

Here was another field opened up to my curiosity which I would have liked very much to explore by further questioning, but my outfitter did his work expeditiously and lunch was waiting. At the table I introduced the subject and asked why the manufacture of cloth by machinery was prohibited in the Iron Republic.

"We prohibit the use of machinery in the making of cloth," answered my host, "for the same reason that we do in the manufacture of everything else that the people can supply without the aid of machinery: that is, that there may be work for all."

---

[1] Revenue or profit taken by a government from the issuing or minting of currency, typically the difference between the face value of the currency and its cost of production.

ch. ends p. 111

"Do I understand that you have no manufactures at all?" I asked.

"Not that we have none at all, but none for the manufacture of any article that can be applied on sufficient quantity to meet the demand, without the use of machinery. This list includes fabrics of almost every description, shoes, hats, head wear, furniture, rope, agricultural implements and products, vehicles, in fact almost everything that we use."

"And the purpose of this is that there may be work for all to do?"

"That is the purpose," replied my host, "and the purpose is accomplished, for as it requires the work of all to supply the wants of all, there is no enforced idleness in this republic."

"But," said I, with a disposition to argue every point, "one man with a machine can do the work of a hundred and it seems to me that with your admirable political conditions, you might well employ the use of machinery, thereby giving the people more time for recreation and the improvement of the mind."

"Certainly there is great temptation to use a machine that will do the work of a hundred men," replied my host, "and if the hundred men were the beneficiaries of its efficiency, there could be no excuse for not using it. You employ labor saving machinery in the United States, and where it does the work of a hundred or a thousand men do they get the benefit of it?"

I could not say that they did.

"As a matter of fact," continued my host, "does anybody derive any benefit except the owners of the machine?" I was obliged to confess that they were the only direct beneficiaries, but that the cost of production was lessened, which of course, must be to the advantage of all.

"Ah, my friend!" exclaimed the professor, "I very much fear that your argument is influenced by your legal training, for it is palpably one sided, being predicated on the assumption that a machine doing the work of a hundred men lessens the price of its products without diminishing the purchasing power of the hundred men who have been deprived of work by it. Now, let us come down to practical illustration. You use machinery in the manufacture of shoes; to what extent does it lessen labor and cost?"

"Very much indeed," I answered warming up to the advantage I thought I saw. "With improved machinery and a division of labor. I have been informed that a man can make a pair of shoes every seven minutes, at a cost of thirty cents."

"Very well; if you are not positive though as to the accuracy of your data, we will allow some latitude and say they make a pair in twelve minutes, at a cost of fifty cents. That will be fifty pairs in a day of ten hours. Your man with the machine then has done the work of fifty men. What pay does he receive?"

"From the best of my information an average of about two dollars per pay," I replied. "Your man is paid two dollars a day and turns out a product that sells for $25 in—"

"Oh no!" I interrupted, "that costs $25 to make."

"I see," said my host smiling,"this is the cost of making. Now what do these shoes sell for?"

"I should say an average of $1.50."

"Ah! Then this man does the work of fifty men and turns out a product that is worth $100 more than the cost of production. Who gets this $100?" asked my host laying down his fork and looking across the table at me with an air of affected simplicity.

"The man or company that owns the machine, I suppose," I answered slightly nettled.

"Then the forty-nine men whose work has been done for them do not come in except in the matter of increased time for recreation! But what surprises me most," my host went on, "is that these shoes can be made for fifty cents and sold for $1.50. How is this feat so contrary to the laws of competition accomplished?"

"In the first place," I answered, "our manufacturers combine to maintain prices among themselves and in the second place

ch. ends p. 111

we have a tariff which brings the imported article up to that price."

"So!" exclaimed my host, "I begin to comprehend your system which I presume was the same when I left the country, but as I was quite a young man and had never paid much attention to such matters. I retain no knowledge on the subject. Now let us look into this system in its practical application. Here is a machine that in one day with the application of one man's labor does the work of fifty men, thereby depriving forty-nine men of the opportunity to work. In the value of the product it turns out, it earns the wages of fifty men and yet all that labor gets out of it is the paltry sum of $2 or not enough to pay for the result of fifteen minutes of its time, the balance going to the owner of the machine. So while flesh and blood and brains and skill earns $2 for labor, wood and iron and steel earns $50 for capital! And this wonderful machine too, in all probability, is the product of skill and labor at the same miserable wage! Is this system conducive to an equitable distribution of wealth among the people? Does it not rather impoverish the forty-nine men whose work is done by the machine and enrich one man who gets the value of fifty men's work for the price of one?"

I could not deny so logical a conclusion.

"Now, in the Iron Republic," continued the professor, "where machinery is not allowed to supplant labor, to produce fifty pairs of shoes in one day would probably require the work of fifty men and the value of their product would be divided among them. So the question resolves itself into this proposition; which is better, to let fifty men earn one dollar apiece, or to let two men earn $100, (one of whom works while the other keeps books), of which amount the working man gets $2 while the bookkeeper gets the balance?"

The proposition did not admit of debate, but I could not refrain from remarking that it seemed a pity that fifty men should labor a day to accomplish what an inanimate machine might do without toil or fatigue.

"Not necessarily," retorted my host. "In appearance and according to the ethics of industrial economy, there could be no objection to the machine doing the work of fifty men if the fifty men got the benefit of its work. And yet it is contrary to the Divine economy, as expressed in the Biblical injunction that man shall eat bread by the sweat of his brow, and like every other human practice that runs contrary to the Divine order, is harmful in its results and I think your system must demonstrate it. Notwithstanding the use of machinery, you doubtless have a large number of men who are steadily and permanently employed; now which makes the best showing, mentally and morally, this steadily employed class, or the unemployed or partially employed class whose time for recreation and the improvement of the mind has been increased by the use of machinery?"

I was compelled to confess that the employed class took precedence both in point of intelligence and morals, I remarked too, that it was a disappointing fact that our public libraries, night schools, and other institutions founded for the benefit and elevation of the masses were least patronized by those of most leisure.

"It is not strange," said my host. "The reasonable employment of the body prepares the mind for recreation. A man's mind though, especially if it be not well cultivated, having nothing to employ it but recreation, grows bad just as most boys do who have nothing to do but play. The universe is founded on a plan and that plan contemplates that every man shall work. The man who does not suffers, and society suffers by him. There are no exceptions to this rule."

"I confess that you have had the better of me all along," said I, "but you are certainly mistaken when you say that there are no exceptions to this rule, for many of our most intelligent and virtuous men are those who have grown vastly rich from the results of other men's labor. I may say most generous also, for in my country hundreds of churches, colleges, libraries, and

ch. ends p. 111

other beneficent institutions stand as monuments to this virtue in them today."

"Undoubtedly," assented the professor, "and yet I must remind you in the first place that a man who becomes a millionaire from the increment of other men's labor can be no idler, for the mere keeping up with his business and getting the lion's, tiger's, and wolf's share of the product of the labor employed by him will keep him busy. And in the second place, when a man makes gifts with money obtained that way, is such generosity in any manner different from that of Robin Hood, who robbed one class and gave to another? Is it even as commendable, for the old highwayman invariably took from the rich and gave to the poor, at the worst doing evil that good might come by contributing to the equalization of wealth, while your millionaires take from the poor and give in such a way as to enhance their reputation, this being the only thing to be desired after having acquired more money than they can use in promoting their pleasures. From my point of view, there is no more generosity in such actions than there was in Trajan's lavish expenditure on his tomb.[2] I think you will find too, that the sons of these millionaires who inherit the money without the training that came with its accumulation will suffer and make society suffer, thus proving the old Bible doctrine that the sins of the parents are visited on the children unto the third and fourth generation."[3]

"That doctrine may be true in theory," I replied laughing, "but in my country the first generation usually exhausts the possibility of the evil by getting rid of the root of it."

"In as far as the money itself may contribute directly to the evil," assented my host, "but a life of profligacy and dissipation made possible by inherited wealth may leave a train of evils behind it extending to generations unborn."

[2] Trajan (53–117) was a Roman soldier-emperor who presided over one of the greatest military expansions in Roman history and led the empire to attain its greatest territorial extent by the time of his death. His ashes were entombed in a small room beneath Trajan's Column, erected to commemorate Trajan's victory in the Dacian Wars.

[3] Deuteronomy 5:9

"Then you regard wealth as an evil, do you?" I asked.

"I certainly regard wealth as a most prolific source of evil and where it is acquired in the manner we have been discussing, that is, where a poor man is required to make shoes for a rich man for fifty cents and then pay $1.50 for the same shoes for himself and family to wear, it is an evil per se. You say this is partly the result of legislation and if it is, yours is a government of the minority, for there must be fewer rich, than poor men."

"I grant what you say," I replied. "Government is of, for, and by the rich, always has been and probably always will be, because wealth is power. But it does not necessarily follow that for that reason it is bad. In the cooperation of mind and matter in the affairs of human government as in everything else, mind must predominate. In predominating, it secures the conditions of life most favorable to itself and thus extends its sphere, as in an exploring party a few men by getting more than their share of food are enabled to penetrate faster and further than their comrades. But as they blaze the way they open up, it is easier for the rest to follow; and so I believe the world has been the gainer by the very inequalities and injustice, which you condemn. In its age-long and worldwide advance, the human mind has not marched in a phalanx.[4] Under favoring conditions the strongest and boldest have broken away and led the advance, scaling walls to others impregnable and climbing heights inaccessible to the average and placing beacon lights to make the ascent easier for those that follow."

"My dear sir," exclaimed the professor, "your figure is very pretty, but I think it is so only because of the beautiful words in which you have clothed it. Skill in the art of dressing may be made to hide many defects," (with a sly glance at the ladies,) "but I am not going to be taken in by mere external appearances. It is not your figure I find fault with but your logic. Let

---

[4] A body of people, usually officers or troops, standing or moving in close formation.

ch. ends p. 111

us state your proposition in the form of a syllogism[5] and proceed logically. Major premise: In its advancement, mind will secure to itself the conditions most favorable to its expansion; minor premise: but wealth is most favorable to the expansion of the mind; conclusion: it is therefore by the aid of wealth that the human mind has advanced to its present wonderful stage of development. Is this a fair and logical statement of the proposition?"

I admitted that it was.

"Very well; then I dispute your minor premise and deny your conclusion," said my host positively. "Wealth is not favorable to the expansion of the mind and for its wonderful development it acknowledges no financial obligation whatsoever. Under the patronage of wealth which was to be the gainer by its product, mind has wrought some of its most beautiful creations and in modern times wealth has supplied in some instances tools to facilitate its work; but in the main, money has rather been the enemy of mind, and wealth, whether supporting monarchical extravagance, religious bigotry, or personal vanity and ambition, has tended to suppress rather than promote the highest and noblest qualities of the human mind. Its sublimest efforts have been achieved in poverty, in exile, in dungeons even, and as for scaling walls impregnable and climbing heights inaccessible, and planting beacon lights for others, as per your pretty figure, the most gifted men have gone to the stake or scaffold, because power, which has always been synonymous with wealth did not approve."

I began to get warm in the collar, for though I had engaged in the discussion more for information than argument, the ease and skill with which my opponent had met and defeated me at every point, aroused all of the belligerency of my nature. But

[5] A form of deductive reasoning in which a conclusion is derived from major and minor premises, each of which shares a term with the conclusion (All A is C; all B is A; therefore, all B is C.)

what made it more exasperating too, the ladies seemed to be deeply interested listeners and caught every point.

"Since you have appealed to Caesar," said I, "unto Caesar will we go. If you resort to logic, I will meet you with your own weapon and state another syllogism for you to disprove. Major premise; in all times wealth and power have been used to repress and retard the development of the mind; minor premise, but it is in the nature of mind to resist oppression and its mightiest energies have been aroused in this resistance; conclusion; therefore wealth and power have unwittingly contributed to the development and expansion of the mind!"

"Very neatly turned!" cried the professor, while the ladies smiled and Miss Helen even infringed the neutrality law's by clapping her hands. "Then your position," continued my host, "is that everything which opposes the advancement of the mind really facilitates its development?"

"Not precisely. Everything which arouses the resistance and overcoming instinct of the mind," I returned.

"The point is well taken and strongly stated," conceded the professor, "but, what wealth and power has contributed to the development of the mind by such direct oppression as to arouse resistance and wake its slumbering energies is slight in comparison with the blight and stagnation induced by war, financial oppression, and industrial wrongs."

"You charge these things to wealth, then?"

"I do, most unqualifiedly," responded my host. "Homer would have us believe that the Trojan War was fought for love, but the wars of history have been for wealth and power."

"I make the point on you," I returned, "that the poorest nations have been the least intelligent and that industrial wrongs have always been greatest where ignorance has been grossest. I think that history will sustain me in the further assertion, that war has been the great civilizer of the world."

"Incontrovertible statements, all," asserted my opponent, "and incorrect only as they confuse cause and effect; if the

ch. ends p. 111

poorest nations have been the least intelligent, they were the poorest because they were the least intelligent and not unintelligent because they were poor. If industrial wrongs have been greatest where ignorance has been most dense, it is simply because the people being ignorant were least able to defend themselves against industrial wrongs. If civilization has been a product of war, it is a byproduct and resulted because, notwithstanding the barbarity and inhumanity of the wars, they brought different peoples together and the knowledge of different nations, by amalgamation,[6] was enlarged. War itself is debasing to the human mind."

"I take issue with you on that," said I hotly. "War may be destructive but it is not debasing. War may be cruel, but cruelty calls forth nobility. War may make widows and orphans, but it also makes heroes, and liberty and patriotism have been fructified by all the blood the earth has ever drunk!"

"And what has been the liberty of the world," my friend asked scornfully, "but the illusion which people cherish when they have exchanged one set of masters for another? And what is the patriotism of the world but that savage and senseless prejudice which is cultivated by teaching the fools of nation to hate the fools of other nations? And when the fools of two nations have been set by the ears by their rulers, they fight and maim and kill—and this is called glorious war!"

"I beg a truce!" I cried, seeing that my venerable host felt deeply on the subject, while I was merely endeavoring to hold up my end of the argument. "I find that I am no match for you Iron Republicans. I have only encountered these accomplished ladies, yourself, and Professor Hallam, and on the subjects of dress, industrial economy, and music I find that I know nothing; am eliminated, obliterated. In other words, to use an Americanism, I am not in it, and hereby surrender:

---

[6] The action, process, or result of uniting or combining.

foot, horse, and dragoons.[7] I cannot offer you my sword for I presume there is no such thing in this model republic."

"They were all beaten into plow-shares[8] long since," answered my friend smiling good humoredly, "so that formality will have to be dispensed with. I am generous though in victory and will pay you the compliment to say that if your cause was worthy of your prowess, the result might be different. In all contests though, the justice of a cause is not less an element of strength than the greatness of cannon and sharpness of steel."

I bowed my acknowledgment of the compliment and indulged the hope that I might yet find some vulnerable point in the Iron Republic, if for nothing else than to redeem myself in the fair eyes that had witnessed my discomfiture.

"I think you are entirely too magnanimous in professing defeat," said Miss Morris, taking part in the conversation for the first time and looking at me with her beautiful eyes beaming with interest. "If you are not too proud to accept an humble ally—"

I bowed again.

"—I venture to suggest that the enemy," (smiling and flashing a glance at her father,) "may attribute his victory—if indeed he has won it—to the fact that the fighting was all in his own territory where he was entrenched. It is my opinion, if I am worthy to be admitted to a council of war, that you run up the white flag too soon."

"With the glorious prospect such a promising alliance opens up to me," I replied facetiously but with a peculiar thrill of gratification, "I hasten to pull down the flag of defeat and beg that you will advance into the breach."

"Well," said my fair ally, "I reopen the attack by the assertion that it was not alone in bringing the nations into closer intercourse that war has exerted a civilizing and elevating influence

[7] Members of European cavalry regiments trained and armed to fight mounted or on foot.

[8] The primary cutting blades of a plow.

ch. ends p. 111

on the human mind. I believe that the highest and noblest thoughts of the peaceful present, owe their origin to the high and noble deeds of a past made glorious by war."

"Tut-tut," exclaimed her father, "the romances of history and Sir Walter Scott[9] have corrupted your mind."

"Kindled rather," retorted my ally with a vigor that proved she was in earnest. "I acknowledge my indebtedness to history and Sir Walter and when I read of the deeds of Couer de Lion[10] and Ivanhoe,[11] even of Dalgetty[12] and De Bracy,[13] I cannot abide the goody goodliness of a big nation like this that works and eats and slumbers like an ox. What would be the history of the world today if the Iron Republic had been founded on the Babylonian empire and its principles had received worldwide acceptances? Try to think of a history of the world without an Alexander or Caesar or Frederick the Great,[14] or Bonaparte or Washington. Without a Marathon[15] or Thermopylae,[16] without Crusades or Couer de Lion!"

I was surprised at the energy with which these words were

[9] Sir Walter Scott (1771-1832) was a Scottish historian, novelist, poet, and playwright who had a major impact on European and American literature.

[10] Richard I (1157-1199), known as Richard Coeur de Lion or Richard the Lionheart because of his reputation as a great military leader and warrior, was King of England; Duke of Normandy, Aquitaine, and Gascony; Lord of Cyprus; Count of Poitiers, Anjou, Maine, and Nantes; and overlord of Brittany.

[11] *Ivanhoe: A Romance* by Sir Walter Scott is an 1819 historical novel published in three volumes.

[12] *A Legend of Montrose* is an 1819 historical novel by Sir Walter Scott, wherein a large section of the novel is taken up with a subplot involving an expedition into enemy territory by the character Dugald Dalgetty.

[13] Maurice de Bracy is one of *Ivanhoe*'s likable villains.

[14] Frederick II (1712-1786), known as Frederick the Great and nicknamed "Old Fritz," was King in Prussia from 1740 until 1772, and King of Prussia from 1772 until his death in 1786.

[15] The Battle of Marathon took place in 490 BC during the first Persian invasion of Greece. The battle was the culmination of the first attempt by Persia, under King Darius I, to subjugate Greece, but the Greek army inflicted a crushing defeat, marking a turning point in the Greco-Persian Wars.

[16] The Battle of Thermopylae was fought in 480 BC between the Persian Empire under Xerxes I and an alliance of Greek city-states led by Sparta under Leonidas I. Lasting over the course of three days, it was one of the most prominent battles of both the second Persian invasion of Greece and the wider Greco-Persian Wars.

uttered and suspected that the strong feeling that prompted them must have been long repressed. My host looked astonished and Mrs. Morris turned to her daughter with a glance of concern as though she had suddenly discovered in her traces of insanity.

"The history of the world, my dear," said her father after a moment's silence, "we may not alter or amend and perhaps would not if we could. It is with the world's life as with a man's: the excesses, dissipations, and sins of early years cannot be blotted out and the experience of them may even serve to enhance the virtues of maturer age. Sometimes such experiences become the foundation of a nobler and more purposeful life and then they may be recalled without regret. But it is a poor life that does not improve with age and the world's life will be unrounded and incomplete if it is not profited by the knowledge and experience of the past."

It is not in me to controvert these words so seriously and truly spoken, but with my new ally, I was in the predicament of the man in the Indian fable, who made an alliance with the tiger and found, after he had bound himself with thongs to that unconquerable beast, that he could not run away when he would.[17]

"I trust you will not be angry with me father, if I seem to dispute with you," replied Miss Helen with unyielding firmness, "but can that have been wholly bad in the past, which is the source of all that is most beautiful in the present? What is the inspiration of poetry and all great thoughts but the high deeds which you impute to the recklessness of the world's youth? War is cruel, but does not its very cruelty provoke nobler sacrifices— as Mr. Barrington has said—and a more exalted heroism than the piping herdsmen of Utopia ever dreamed of? And may it not be in the plan of creation that sunshine and storm, tears and

---

[17] A reference to the popular Indian folktale *The Tiger, the Brahmin, and the Jackal.*

ch. ends next p.

laughter, love and hate, war and peace, shall alternate like day and night to the end of time?"

"My daughter," answered her father gravely, "I am grieved at the low estimation in which you seem to hold your country, and that condition which has been the desire of the ages, but you are entitled to your opinions and I would not have you repress them in deference to me. It is my faith though, that the plan of creation contemplates the ultimate elimination of hate and strife and all evil whatsoever. And though he may not appeal to youth and a romantic imagination, the piping herdsmen of Utopia, who tends his flocks and lives in peace, with clean hands and an upright heart, is to me, a nobler example of God's creation than any medieval swashbuckler that ever drew sword or broke lance to win the silly fancy of a foolish lady love. To my mind, Professor Hallam, who would walk around a block rather than tread upon a worm, is a greater man than Couer de Lion ever was, from every intelligent point of view."

"It may be wrong and wicked," cried the beautiful woman vehemently, with flashing eyes and flushed face, "and if it is I can't help it and I don't care; but I am tired to death of this dreary monotony of peace and prosperity, and the ring of a spearhead upon a breastplate or the clash of swords in a glorious cause would make sweeter music for me than all the piping herdsmen of Utopia—or all the fiddlers of Ironia, for that matter," and bursting into tears she rose hastily from the table and left the room.

"Well I'll declare!" exclaimed my host pushing back his chair. "Who can solve the female enigma?"

I could not, but the one under consideration had gratified me exceedingly by her strange conduct, though I could not tell exactly why. It is said that women are past finding out and I have never been a careful investigator, but without understanding it, the contemptuous reference to the "fiddlers of Ironia" braced me up immensely.

With a woman's penetration, probably, Mrs. Morris saw

further into the matter than any of us and saying something about girls heads being filled with romance she left the table also and followed her daughter from the room. The meal had been concluded some time before, and as Miss Morris' unexpected denouement— if the word may be used here—had very naturally put an end to the conversation, my host led the way and we adjourned to the library.

CHAPTER 10

Ten or fifteen minutes after leaving the dining room we were made aware by the ringing of a gong that the carriage had arrived and, looking out, I saw a handsome vehicle with two seats, besides the driver's, standing at the door. My host called for the ladies and they came down immediately. Miss Helen blushed as she entered the room and approaching her father with downcast eyes, kissed him on the cheek.

"How now, my young renegade, what means this treason to your country?" he exclaimed holding' her face between his hands and looking at her with mock severity.

"It simply means that the country is all right, *Ma Pere*,[1] but that I am not ready for the millennium," she replied smiling faintly and with that she turned on me a glance that made my heart bound and I mentally snapped my fingers at the "fiddlers of Ironia." There was something in that glance which said plainer than words that there was a bond between us and the alliance would be continued. She was attired for the drive in a blue flannel gown buttoned to the throat like an English riding habit, with jaunty cap and gloves to match. Her mother was

---

[1] Translated from French: My father.

similarly dressed in a dark brown suit, and without delay we passed out to the carriage.

As we stood by the carriage, while my host was giving the motorman directions as to the course of the drive, Mrs. Morris remarked that I had best sit on the back seat with the professor, as looking forward gave a better opportunity for observation. The seats faced each other and whether it was by accident or design (I hoped the latter), her mother had no sooner spoken the words than Miss Helen stepped forward and placed her foot on the step to enter the carriage. I helped her in and her mother after her and then at another lightning like flash of those wonderful eyes which conveyed more meaning than any mere words, I entered the carriage and took my seat opposite to her. Professor Morris followed taking his seat by my side and as I looked into the face of the peerless woman before me, so chaste and beautiful, with just the suggestion of a fine scorn in the curve of the exquisitely chiseled mouth and drooping eyelids, I felt that but for the presence of others, I must have fallen on my knees before her. If Cupid had let me pass through all the years before unscathed, he was atoning for his dereliction by a most extraordinary display of archery, for with every glance of those glorious eyes an arrow seemed to quiver in my heart. Never having experienced the sentiment, sensation—or whatever it is—of love, my resources in that direction were untouched and I came to it like a strong man to a race. I had known this woman less than two days and already I felt as if I had known and loved her for years, so impressed upon my heart was every feature of her face and every speaking glance of those marvelous unfathomable eyes. Indeed, by some strange consciousness it began to dawn upon me that I had looked upon that face and into those eyes before. Was there truth in the theosophical philosophy of Plato, or had I seen her in a dream? It seemed incredible to me that I had looked upon her for the first time, only the day before. It could not be!

I could not in so short a time have become so familiar with every lineament and every changing expression of quick intelligence.

When we left my friend's door, we did not go toward the capitol but in another direction, through streets I had not seen before. The houses were unpretentious as a rule, built of brick and stone mostly and everywhere there was an appearance of comfort without ostentation. We passed through miles of shaded streets, by fountains and monuments, through parks and pleasure grounds, finding everywhere beauty, cleanliness, and evidences of prosperity. We passed houses of the most distinguished men of the nation, including those of the president, members of the Supreme Cabinet, and others eminent for their achievements in the field of science and letters, and there was no noticeable difference between them and the residences of ordinary citizens. There seemed to be no aristocratic quarter and when I proposed to turn through the slums and succeeded in making myself understood. I was informed that there was no slums and nothing corresponding to them.

"Have you then reached that ideal social state where you have no poor?" I asked.

"We have at least reached that ideal social state where we have no rich," answered the professor.

"Indeed! Do you mean to say that you have no wealthy class at all?"

"More," replied my host, "that we have no wealthy person at all."

"What!" I exclaimed. "Not a single rich man in the entire Republic?

"Not a single rich man, woman, or child in the entire Republic and never can be," was the answer.

"I shall not argue about this," I remarked after a few minutes reflection, "and whether or not it is a desirable condition, it is certainly a peculiar one for a country like this, that seems to be blessed, not only with material resources of every description, but with the skill and energy to utilize them to the last degree.

ch. ends p. 130

Will you explain to me why it is that in such a country a man of industry and good judgment does not grow rich as elsewhere in the world."

"For the same reason that a man does not lift himself over a stile[2] by the straps of his boots," answered the professor facetiously. "Simply because it is a feat impossible of accomplishment."

"But why? The conditions seem to be most favorable."

"In the first place," said the professor, "if it were not for debt, interest and unearned increment, men could not become rich even where they are not restrained; and in the second place, here, where we have none of these evils, we anticipate the possibility of such a thing by legislation which renders it impossible."

"But that is what I wish to understand: how do you evade these evils—as you call them—on the one hand and anticipate them on the other?"

"Well," replied the professor, "besides having no debt, interest, or unearned increment, which condition itself is a bar to wealth, we have a graduated income tax which would reach the point of confiscation before even moderate wealth, according to your standards, is attained. For instance, all incomes above 800 diems are taxed ten percent, and ten percent, for every additional four hundred diems, which limits the income to forty four hundred diems, for at that point the tax takes the whole. You see this tax limits income to a possible sum of twelve hundred diems."

"But," said I, "without asking it argumentatively, how can you, who are such a stickler for justice in the abstract, justify this confiscation of a man's property, when, as you claim, your system is so perfect that it cannot be acquired by dishonest methods?"

"Theoretically, it is unjust," assented the professor, "but the object of a truly enlightened government is not so much

---

[2] A series of steps or rungs in a wall or fence constructed so as to allow humans, but not animals, to pass over.

to vindicate any ethical code, as to secure the happiness and welfare of its citizens. If a particular bull should grow horns so much longer than the rest of the herd as to put it at its mercy, he should be dehorned although it might seem cruel! Not because he had acquired his weapons unjustly, but because having them puts it in his power to be unjust. We have ideal political conditions and I cannot conceive how a man with any amount of money here could use it to the detriment of others, but you remember Alexander's boast that no city was impregnable to him, into which he could introduce an ass laden with gold."

"When you stated just now that you had no such things as debt, interest, and unearned increment," I remarked, "I take it that you intended to convey the idea that these were practical nullities above the limit fixed by your income tax. Below that limit I presume a man may use his money in the way that will yield the largest returns."

"He may use it in any legitimate way," was the answer. "That is, he may buy commodities or employ labor or engage in any enterprise that does not conflict with the statutes. My statement though was absolutely true; there is no such thing as debt, interest, and unearned increment even in the most limited sense."

"Then you have no credit system at all?" I asked.

"Our people do not know the meaning of the word credit when applied to commercial transactions," replied the professor. "A man cannot become a debtor or creditor because the law does not recognize any such conditions. The nearest approach to it is the binding force of contracts, but the statutes have been so carefully framed that the obligations of contracts cannot be made to partake of the nature of debt. There being no such thing as debt, there can of course be no such thing as interest. And as by the national exchange system, nothing can be sold for more than the average cost of production, one man cannot make much money off of another man's labor."

"It seems then, that one object of your government is to keep the people poor!"

ch. ends p. 130

"The object," answered the professor, "is not to keep the people poor, but to keep them in such a condition of equality that one class cannot take advantage of another, but wealth and poverty are purely relative terms and it cannot be said that the object is anymore to keep them all poor than to make them all rich. And when I said that we had no rich people. I meant according to your standard and that of the old world. In the truest sense, our people are for the most part all rich, having a country abounding with resources of every kind which have been utilized, and being protected from taxes, interest, and every form of oppression that could rob them of the fruits of their labor."

"And do you mean to say that you have no taxes either?" I asked incredulously.

"Practically none," my friend answered. "We have a graduated income tax, but only in theory as there is no opportunity for its application and it was only enacted to guard against unforeseen contingencies. There is a tax, too, on all unused land of five percent, of what it is capable of producing that being what the state would get from it if it was cultivated. But as this results in the government owning all of the unused land and as any citizen can take possession of and hold all that he can use, free of charge to himself his heirs and assigns forever, that tax is practically inoperative."

"Really," I exclaimed, "the more I learn of this wonderful country, the more I am amazed! But if you have no taxes tell me how this model government is supported."

"The Bureau of Subsistence and the Department of Public Utilities supply the means necessary for the expenses of the government," answered the professor.

"Will you explain to me how this is done?" I asked. "It certainly must be a very complicated system."

"On the contrary," replied the professor, "it is so extremely simple that every merchant and farmer in your country puts it in practice in the conduct of his business. Freight and passenger tariffs on the railroads, canals, and navigable rivers—and lighting, power, telephone, and express services and franchises yield the department of public utilities a sufficient sum, together with the profits derived from the national exchange system, to meet all the expenses of government."

"I see," said I. "The profits of all this business go to the government."

"Yes, to the government," answered my friend, "for to use a fiction of this kind is a convenient way to express the aggregate ownership of the people."

"I can see but one difficulty," I remarked, "and that is in adjusting these tariffs and profits as it is impossible to tell what they will yield."

"That presents no difficulties," was the reply, "as the tariffs and percentages for the ensuing year are based on the expenses of the government the year before. For instance, the total cost of operating the government last year was about two hundred million diems of which about five and a half millions are used in defraying the expenses of the government proper, and the balance in operating its exchanges and utilities. Assuming that the business of these departments will be the same this year as last, it is a simple arithmetical problem to fix the tariffs to raise the necessary amount. As a matter of fact though, in making up the budget for any year, a very liberal margin is allowed and the excess thus accruing is expended by the department of progression in scientific experimentation and new utilities."

"You say the actual cost of government last year, outside of running your railroads, exchanges, and other utilities was about five and a half million diems. What is a diem?"

"It is the value of a day's work and is the unit of our financial system. It is about the value of an American dollar."

"And what is the population of the Republic?"

"A little over fifty million."

"It seems incredible," said I, "that fifty million people can be governed for this sum and——"

ch. ends p. 130

"Say served for this sum!" interrupted the professor.

"Well served for that sum and I cannot understand it in any other light than that your people have advanced to a higher plane of intelligence and morality than the people of other countries."

"It may be said without egotism that they have advanced to a somewhat higher plane of intelligence," said the professor, "for the results of it are here to show, but I do not think they are any better morally. Morality and religion is the surplus crop here, as in America and everywhere else. They do not rob and oppress because they have combined for mutual protection against each other."

"The entire government seems to be run on the principles of a great trust or corporation," I remarked.

"That's just exactly what it is," replied my friend. It is the logical end and culmination of trusts and monopoly. It is a trust formed of the whole people for purposes of government, commerce, transportation, education, and everything else that pertains to their welfare. The cost of the entire system in all its branches, operative, legislative, judicial, educational, and penal amounts to an impost[3] of about five percent on commerce, while the tariffs for transportation and other public utilities probably does not exceed one-half of what they are in countries dominated by wealth."

I had never had any commercial training, but I knew that it cost all the way from ten to one hundred percent of the value of any product in the United States to get it out of the hands of the producer and into those of the consumer. "What is the total business of this vast trust in all branches?" I asked.

"Something like four billion diems," replied the professor.

Fifty million people in one great trust! And that so organized and safeguarded that no member could ever take advantage of another. I could scarcely conceive of such a thing, but it

[3] Tax.

was extremely simple in theory and there it was, in successful operation right before my eyes.

"I am beginning to comprehend something of your wonderful scheme of government," I remarked, "but as one of the first things I learned after leaving my ship was that you do not use metal money as a medium of exchange. I am curious to learn something of your financial system. How does your medium of exchange originate and on what is it based?"

"I believe," said the professor, without answering my question, "that our financial system is as near perfect as anything of human origin can be."

"And do you not think your whole governmental scheme is perfect?" I asked in surprise.

"No, indeed," replied my friend. "It is ideal in comparison with what has been accomplished in the world before, but the final perfect government is no government at all."

"Why Professor, you cannot mean anarchy!" I exclaimed.

"Oh, no," he answered, "just no government. When people become fully civilized and Christianized, and that narrow delusion called patriotism gives place to worldwide fraternalism, there will be no necessity for government or laws."

"For goodness sake," I cried, "leave something for heaven and hereafter! But this monetary system, tell me something about that."

"It is all comprehended in these propositions," said the professor. "The value of anything is what it is worth to man; and it is honestly worth to one man what it costs another man to produce it. Value in a medium of exchange can only inhere[4] when that medium is a commodity of intrinsic worth, or when it represents such a commodity, and then its value is exactly that of the article it represents."

"Very well, go on."

"Where there are no exchangeable commodities of value,

---

[4] To be inherent; exist essentially or permanently in.

ch. ends p. 130

there can be no honest medium of exchange because there is no exchangeable commodity for it to represent. Here, the value of everything is based on the average cost of production, and when it passes out of the hands of the producer, he is entitled to its value in anything else he may want. In a crude state of society this exchange is effected by bartering one article for the other directly, or by converting them into pieces of metal or other unscientific forms of 'money' of uncertain or arbitrary value and using it as a medium of exchange. But as this medium is an uncertain quantity, depending on the discovery of mines, the vagaries of legislation, and the manipulation of the financiers who own and control it, commerce in all commodities becomes a mere shuttlecock in the hands of the money masters, and the value of everything, in their medium, is subject to their will. Under such conditions, it is not strange that in a country where plenty is produced for all, a few roll in wealth and luxury while many suffer for the actual comforts of life. It is not strange either, that those who control the money are the ones that roll in wealth, while those who do all the work and produce all of the commodities grovel in want. This is the result of ignorance on the part of the producing masses and is about on a par with that fabled transaction in which were concerned two cats, a monkey, and a piece of cheese.[5] In the place of that crude and unjust system, the Iron Republic employs a scientific method that is just to all. The value of every product is scientifically fixed by the average cost of production, and when a man produces anything he delivers it to the great popular trust called the government and receives therefore its assiento,[6] which are certificates of its value and deposit. As everything that is produced is placed in escrow just the same, these assiento are

---

[5] One of Aesop's Fables. The title varies according to the source, but is generally styled as "Two Cats and a Monkey." The gist being: Two cats unable to agree on how to divide it, let a monkey split their stolen cheese. The monkey cuts odd pieces, then eats the difference trying to make them equal, before eating the last small piece as his fee. The moral being: When you argue, someone else gains.

[6] A Spanish word meaning seat, contract, or agreement.

exchangeable for any other commodity on the same basis of value. These assiento then, are the circulating medium and not a diem of them can exist outside of the national exchange unless its value in some commodity exists within it. As long as there is a diem's worth of any commodity in the hands of the government exchange, there is outstanding, somewhere, a diem to represent that commodity. When that commodity is withdrawn for consumption the diem is absorbed by the government and the financial incident is closed. These assiento are numbered and dated and must go through the exchange once a year, either in exchange for commodities or new assiento, (they are re-issued every year), so if any are lost or destroyed, after the date of the annual funding they are made good to the loser, if he has preserved the numbers so that his loss can be identified. Under this system no great store of money can be hoarded anywhere, and there is no temptation in that direction as it cannot be made to yield interest or increment. In carrying out this great governmental trust, four billion diem are issued and absorbed annually, and so the great financial tide ebbs and flows with the regularity and certainty of the tides of the ocean. Best of all, no man can receive value until he produces value, and so we have a great human hive in which there are no drones. This may seem to you a small volume of business for so large a nation, but as middlemen are practically eliminated and there is no wasteful competition, a mutual exchange of commodities is effected with much less trading than in your country."

"And have you no merchants at all?" I asked.

"Oh, yes," was the answer, "we have a considerable number of men engaged in supplying the wants of the people, besides those employed at the exchange, but they can hardly be called merchants, as they are in reality caterers. They establish themselves in locations more convenient to the people of certain sections than the exchange and receive a small advance over the exchange prices merely on account of that convenience. The exchange fixes the price, though, of everything and the

ch. ends p. 130

caterers are only paid enough more to pay for this convenience, as the exchange is open for all. Of course this applies only to the commodities that are handled in the exchange: there are many commodities, perishable goods, confectioneries, and an endless variety of gimcracks[7] that are not received into the exchange at all and are dispensed by the caterers."

"Your absolute cash system undoubtedly saves a vast amount of loss and litigation," said I, "but men are compelled to have accommodation or suffer, and that, it seems to me, is where your system would work great hardship."

"If there was no remedy," replied the professor, "it were still better that a few should suffer than many, but the system provides even against this. If a man has nothing he is a pauper, in the language of your country, and could not get accommodation there nor anywhere else. If he has non-perishable property of any kind though, here, he can go to the exchange in his commonwealth and get assiento to the amount of fifty percent of the value of the property without interest. Of course he must give a bond for this value signed by freeholders to protect the exchange against loss."

"Referring to these assiento, is it not possible to counterfeit them?" I asked.

"It might be done," answered the professor, "although they are printed on socially prepared paper, but as every man who passes one may be required to endorse it. It would be like counterfeiting a bank check in your country, which can be done by anybody. The penalty though, is severe, and as we have no idle class, there is no criminal class, and any kind of a misdemeanor is a rare occurrence in this country."

"I should think," I remarked, "that having to endorse these assiento in every small transaction would be annoying."

"They are not used in small transactions," was the reply.

---

[7] Cheap and showy ornaments; knickknacks.

"They may be deposited and converted into fractional currency at any post office."

"Indeed, and what are the denominations of your money?"

"Our lowest denomination is the minum, which represents five minutes labor. Then we have three minutes, six minutes, and the hora, which is supposed to represent an hours work and as a day's work here is eight hours, the hora is worth about twelve and a half cents in your money. Above this, we have the quarter diem, half diem, and diem. In the larger denominations there are one, two, three, five, and ten diems. Money here represents labor and labor is made the basis, or unit, if I may use that term, of its value. Twelve minums make a hora, eight horas make a diem."

While this conversation, so dry and uninteresting to the ordinary reader, was going on, many places of interest were pointed out to me and I was keenly alive to the beauties of the city through which we were rapidly propelled. Afterward we passed out into the country, where on every hand were the same evidences of prosperity I had seen in the city. Modest but comfortable houses, paved roads, every resource of nature taxed to the last degree to sub serve the convenience of man.

"It must have taken a great while," I remarked, "for people to reduce the art of living to this point of perfection."

"On the contrary," replied my friend, "the change was wrought in a very few years. When the people found that it paid to live in this intelligent, scientific way and the spirit of reform got in the air, they went at it with a vim."

We were going through a pleasant, shady lane, on one side of which were some cattle standing under the trees, and on the other, a man plowing in a field with a horse—the first I had seen. We were yet some distance from the farmhouse when hearing a humming noise behind us I looked around and saw a box or a car about as long and thick and about half as wide as a square piano running toward us on two cables stretched on poles. I had noticed these cables and a lot of other wires but

ch. ends p. 130

I had not learned all of their uses. "Here's another new one on me!" I cried, standing up in the carriage to see the thing go by.

"That is the rural express," said the professor, laughing, and then he directed the motorman to keep up with it until we passed the farmhouse that I might have an opportunity to see it work if it should have something to deliver there. It was running about thirty miles an hour and we spurted along by it till it passed the house. The box or carrier ran eight or ten feet above the ground and when it reached a pole in front of the house, one of a number of knobs or cranks that projected from the side of it engaged a pin on the pole and several packages were thrust out of the rear end of it and dropped into a box-like receptacle attached to the pole just below. A gong was rung at the same time and a lady came out of the house, lowered the box with a pulley, and took out the packages. This rural delivery, the professor told me, was one of the newest of the public utilities and was just being introduced. It had proved a success and the Department of Progress intended to put them on throughout the Republic. They were run from the exchanges and post offices and carried, besides mail, packages up to twenty pounds weight. The cables also carried electric light and power currents and the carriers ran in circuits going on round and back to the starting point when empty. Several of them passed us while we were on the line of the circuit and were running continuously. This section of country was an elevated plateau and to the northward could be seen the blue outlines of the Illyrian hills.

The afternoon was perfect with an Indian summer haze, and as we traveled at the rate of about twenty miles an hour we traversed a wide extent of territory. Scenes of Arcadian beauty were spread out everywhere, and as I thought of the miserable hirelings and wage earners of America and the old world, the sweatshops and crowded tenements, the dwarfed and stunted lives that result from the mad struggle for wealth, I said feelingly, "I would to God the poor of my country could come here when they die; it would he heaven to them!"

"What more could heaven be?" exclaimed the professor, stretching out his hand toward the lovely undulating fields. "To live, to labor, and to love! Is that not heaven? Unharrowed by galling apprehension of poverty and want, walking the sweet sequestered vale of life and taking from the hands of all-providing, beneficent nature every good and beautiful thing that can minister to our wants, what more can heaven be than an endless continuation of the same? And this would be the condition of the whole world if men could learn the unwisdom of selfishness or were but wise enough to combine for mutual protection against themselves!"

His wife gazed upon him with affectionate admiration, but the beautiful daughter looked away listlessly as though she were bored with it all. I felt, with a pang of disappointment, that this beautiful woman must after all be shallow and feeling less, but when, a moment later, she turned to me with a wistful look in her eyes and asked me if I did not think that if one had been born in heaven and had never lived anywhere else, they would grow tired of it, I comprehended something of the ennui[8] that made life tiresome to her even in so blessed a country. And again I snapped my fingers at the "fiddlers of Ironia," for said I to myself—although I knew little of the female heart—"no woman would become ennuied with this glorious country if she had really learned to love and the object of her love were here!"

We encountered motorcycles of every description and passed through several shires where the national exchange buildings, post offices, and public schools looked like the buildings of some old barony or monastery of the middle ages, but with what a difference! These people were great and free with no feudal masters to fatten and fight, or shaveling[9] priests to feast and fatten on the fruits of their toil. Each for all and all for each, not because they were more unselfish than their less fortunate

---

[8] Boredom.

[9] An archaic derogatory term for a clergyman or priest with a tonsured head (a tonsure is the shaved crown of the head of a monk or priest).

ch. ends p. 130

fellowmen but because they had learned that only a few could be great and rich, and acting with the wisdom and power that belonged to the majority, they had mutually agreed that none should be rich and none great except in a noble and unselfish way that made the greatness of one the common heritage and pleasure of all.

Making a wide detour, we came to the Urbana river and followed its course back to the city. It was as picturesque as the Hudson but no palaces lined its banks. Modest and unpretending cottages, comfortable and adequate; many of them beautiful in design, but all simple and unostentatious, as though built more for use than to advertise the station of the owner, faced the wide boulevard that ran by the river like the long winding streets of an old fashioned American village. We had reached the great dam only a few miles from the city and stopped to look at the public buildings where the million-horse power of the mighty river was transmuted into that subtle, incomprehensible force that night and day, ran hundreds of miles of railroad, thousands of electric lights, rural express carriers, mills and other public utilities.

"See!" said the professor as the sun touched the horizon, a great ball of fire, "the grand old sun after lighting and warming us all day, will still by this water he has lifted from the sea, work for us all night!" It was beautiful. Far up the river to a distant bend, the water above the dam lay smooth and placid and flashed like silver. On one side, a steep wooded bank descended from the boulevard to the water's edge where were rustic seats and boathouses at intervals along. On the other side a wall of rock, perpendicular in some places, and seamed and serrated like the rough-chased facade of some old giant's castle, rose sheer to the height of nearly a hundred feet, over the edge of which in some places fell great festoons[10] of flowering vines.

"Those lovely banks," said the professor, after I had admired

---

[10] Strings, garlands, ribbons, leaves, or flowers suspended in a loop or curve between two points.

their picturesque beauty, "were once crowned with the villas of the manufacturing, commercial and financial barons of this country. The masses labored for them, the great river toiled for them. Now, where pretentious palaces once vied with each other to advertise their owner's wealth, stand the happy homes of a people who are neither masters nor slaves, and the great river too, is masterless, for lo, it works for all!"

At this moment, the great sun disappeared behind the horizon and as the broad amber bars of light flashed up and expanded like flaming banners in the sky, a deep solemn chime of music came rolling grandly down from toward the city whose outlines could but dimly be discerned against the background of night that loomed behind. On came the music, stately and grand as became the time and scene. Sinking to deep sweet symphonies that seemed to breathe the spirit of blessed contentment and repose anon it swelled to magnificent burst of glorious music that carried a note of exultation and triumph like the exulting pean of a worldwide victory of the ages. Unconsciously I uncovered my head under the spell of the divine nocturne and in every direction as far as I could see, on the boulevard or in boats upon the river, men stopped and listened reverentially as to the Angelus. For ten minutes the glorious strain swelled from the "tower of music," rolled out over the fading landscape, and echoed and reverberated along the walls and cliffs of the winding river. And then ceasing, with flash, ten thousand electric lights punctuated the gathering darkness and the great city gleamed in flashing outline like the realization of a fairy scene in a story of the Arabian Nights.

I looked at my host. His eyes were closed, he sat with such an expression of deep solemnity and peace upon his noble face, that I felt a thrill of awe as though in the presence of an inspired prophet of the olden time. I turned my eyes to the queenly woman that sat before me and the spell had worked not less powerfully on her. Her head was thrown back, her hands were clasped and from her half-closed eyes the tears

ch. ends next p.

were running down her cheeks. That music was a man's soul, the soul of genius, lavishing itself on earth-born clods with such beauty and power as for the moment to make them too, feel that they were divine. And what was I in the presence of a spirit like this? In the exaltation of that moment, so gross a thing as jealousy could not abide and I felt myself a glowworm with the sunshine beating upon me.

"Fiddlers of Ironia!" Never again could I force my lips to frame those words. No one spoke save the motorman, who when the music ceased and the last rhythmic wave was lost in the darkening reaches of the river, uttered a deep "amen," and at a signal from my host, pulled sharply on his lever and we shot away toward the city.

CHAPTER II

The critical reader may observe that the conversation and discussions just recorded are better suited to an industrial congress than a drawing room or carriage ride through a beautiful country in the company of beautiful women. But it must be remembered that the astounding conditions by which I was surrounded were entirely new to me. It was as if a man should be born full grown into the wonders of the 20th century, and as a student and politician my environment impressed me no less by the wherefore than facts of its existence.

When an inquisitive boy gets hold of a mechanical toy, he scarcely awaits to see it operate before going into it to see how it operates. And so, while I was charmed and enthused by my surroundings and interested in my companions, deeply in one of them, the emotion of curiosity was uppermost in my mind. The facts of the existence of amazing facts were broadcast before me everywhere. The wherefore of their existence I was reaching after greedily. If I may use such an expression, the is–ness was like a world bathed in sunlight. The why–ness like cloud drifts breaking over the horizon and floating toward me.

All of us being somewhat fatigued with the long afternoon drive, we sat up only long enough after the evening repast to take a resume of the day and then retired.

The next morning I held a conversation with Captain Brent over the telephone and then took the train for Aegia.

The duties of his office prevented Professor Morris from accompanying me and I anticipated rather a dull ride, but I had no sooner entered my compartment than I discovered that I was in the company of an original character.

"Peace be unto you brother," said he as I took my seat opposite to him in the car.

"The same to you, my friend," I replied, not knowing what else to say.

"Do you live in this God forsaken city of the plain?" he asked waving his hand in a general way toward the world outside.

"Only a temporary sojourner," said I, surprised at his words and the solemn tones of condemnation with which they were uttered.

"Even a temporary sojourn in Sodom will do you hurt my brother," said he sententiously. "Come out from among them and be ye separate!" saith the Holy Book. Lot was only a temporary sojourner in the city of the plain, but if you will read his subsequent history in the Divine Allegory, you will admit that it could not have been any worse with him if he had lived there all his life.[1] These things were written in the Divine Allegory for our guidance in real life and we do well to take heed lest we, too, partake of evil and so bring ruin upon us."

"Sir," I said looking at him in astonishment. "I am a stranger here and I must confess that your language is beyond my comprehension. If I may make bold to ask, who and what are you?"

"I perceive that you are indeed a stranger," remarked the man with an unconscious swell of pride in his voice, "or you would not need to ask that question. I am the voice of one crying in the wilderness 'prepare ye the way of the Lord, make His paths straight!'[2] My name is Moses and I am the founder and head

---

[1] In the Book of Genesis (Chapter 19), Lot's wife, who failed to heed God's command, was turned into a pillar of salt as they fled from the destruction of Sodom and Gomorrah.

[2] Matthew 3:3, Mark 1:3, Luke 3:4.

of the Zionists. Unto us is committed the work of repairing the broken down walls that the people may go in and out in peace. Have you not read the 'Torchlight of Truth'?"

I assured him that I had never seen it.

"Aha!" he cried, clenching his fist and shaking it at the universe at large. "The powers of darkness conspire to keep the light from the people but the truth is mighty and will prevail. Read this (pulling out a newspaper, the first I had seen, from a pile under the seat and handing it to me), and when you have read it change your garments, wash your flesh in pure water, and come into the fellowship of Zion."

I glanced at the paper, which was printed in old English and saw that it was made up like many similar American publications of lamentations, proclamations, and execrations and was against everything in general and the Iron Republic in particular.

"Why is it," I asked, "that you employ newspapers while all other news and general intelligence is diffused by the telephone?"

"Because of a conspiracy, sir, a damnable conspiracy!" pounding his knee with his fist. "In the beginning we put it on the news service, but it was excluded by the Department of Public Utilities on the ground that it monopolized more than half the service while it was demanded by only a few people. And yet, sir, we put on only about one hundred thousand words a day. Think of it, sir, the Divine Truth suppressed because there was much of it and only a few people wanted to hear it! The very reasons why it should have been given even if it monopolized the whole service!"

"I don't quite agree with you there," I interrupted. "As citizens of the Iron Republic as I understand it and contributing to its maintenance, I should say you were entitled to the benefit of the news service in the proportion that your numbers compare with the population of the country at large. No more than that,

ch. ends p. 137

but certainly that much if it is the ideally representative government that it is claimed to be."

"God's curse on the ideally representative government it is claimed to be!" shouted my strange companion violently. "What does it represent, sir? Men, not God! The human and not the Divine! God is the creator of all things in heaven and earth and should rule in both, not men. I am happy to say that Zionists do not contribute to the maintenance of such a government except in so far as they are compelled to by the use of the public utilities. They have things in common and hold themselves aloof from the exchanges so that they cannot be taxed for the support of such an iniquitous Babylon."

"My dear, sir," I remarked quietly. "I am a stranger to you and your creed and do not wish to enter into any discussion, but I cannot conceive how the creator of the world can rule in it except as he does by the laws of nature which seem to me to be inadequate for the government of a civilized state."

"You cannot see how the Creator can rule the world!" he exclaimed. "None are so blind as those who will not see. Read my book on 'Theory of Divine Government!' How did He rule Israel in the Divine Allegory? Was it by voting and drawing lots and putting Smith, Smate, and Smathers in office over His people because they happened to draw their seals out of a wheel? I say no! He called and anointed his servants to rule over His heritage, to give laws, and make His will known to men!"

"Ah!" I exclaimed, catching his drift, "you mean that all rulership should be in the hands of those only who are called and inspired for that purpose."

"That is exactly what I mean," he answered. "If the people are ruled by men who are divinely called to that high function, they must be ruled according to the will of the Supreme Ruler which is the only perfect way."

"But how could we know who were called to these high offices?" I ventured to inquire.

"How did the people know in the Divine Allegory that Moses

and Samuel and Paul and David were called? Because it was revealed to these men and they made it known to the people. How do I know that I have been called to rule this nation in the name of the Lord? Because it has been revealed to me and I must make it known to a stubborn and stiff-necked race, whether they will hear or whether they will forbear. The powers of darkness are leagued against the truth, but the arm of the Lord is not shortened and He will triumph gloriously over His enemies!"

"So!" I mentally ejaculated, "cranks are not the result of environment, but of our common human nature for they breed them even in the Iron Republic.

"My friend," I remarked, not wishing to argue with him as I had had some experience with this genus in America, "I have no controversy with you, being at the present time a student, an humble pupil of any who will teach me, but several times you have referred to a divine allegory. What do you mean by that, the Bible?"

"The Divine Allegory, my brother, is the Holy Word that has been given to man in figures and emblems for his guidance in the stern realities of actual life. It is called the Bible, or Word, and gives us knowledge of the will and relations of the Divine to the human."

"But," I asked, "why do you call it an allegory? Is it not a record of the real facts of God's dealings with man?"

"Why certainly not!" he replied, "that were impossible."

"But why impossible?" I persisted.

"Simply because there is no possible basis for such real facts. Where is your Egypt and Palestine and Jerusalem and Babylon in real life? Where is your Dead Sea and Mount Sinai and Rome and Athens?" And he gave me a look of pitying triumph.

"Where?" I retorted somewhat confused by his confident air, bluffed, as we say in America, "why they are where they have always been, of course. Egypt is in Africa, Palestine is in Asia,

ch. ends next p.

Rome is in Italy, and Athens is in Greece. What's the matter with you anyhow, been eating prunes?"

"So, my brother!" (with a commiserating leer), "do you cover one impossibility with another! Where then is your Africa, Asia, Italy, and Greece?"

"Where are they?" I replied still further confused by his domineering insistence, "why they are where they have always been too, of course."

"Well, my brother, you ask me to teach you and yet you appear to know far more than I do. I have been through every province of the country and have circumnavigated its coast and have failed to find these places or anything answering to them."

"Why man," I exclaimed in amazement, "they are not in the Iron Republic, but on the other side of the world!"

"I tell you I have been all through and all around it," said he contemptuously, "and I repeat they do not exist."

"What!" I asked, being now convinced that the man was daft, "do you mean to say, that there is no world beyond the confines of this Iron Republic?"

"I mean to say that this is the world and if there is any other it has never been discovered."

"Why, my friend," I exclaimed, "your own histories must record the fact that this country was settled by colonists from England as late as the sixteenth century!"

"Lies!" said he snapping his fingers contemptuously. "Scholastic lies to deceive the credulous and make foundation for evil practices. The children of the Truth know better."

"Now see here," I said warming up and getting interested in spite of the whole thing, "you have literature, hundreds of books, histories, philosophies, poems that were written in other countries: how then can you deny their existence?"

"Lies all," he replied waving his hand scornfully as if to brush them out of the way. "All lies, my brother."

"You have had ships and men come here from America

during your lifetime; there are men here now that were born in that country!"

"All lies!" he reiterated. "Cunningly devised fables to deceive the unwary, but the children of the Truth know better."

"The devil! I'm from America myself!"

"Lies, all li——"

"Thunderation!" I cried seizing him by the collar and yanking him out of the seat. "Do you mean to call me a lie?"

"Help! Help!" he shouted lustily, "the man is crazy!"

"You are crazy yourself, you infernal old loon!" I shouted shaking him all over the seats.

"Friends! fellowmen! save me from the clutches of this maniac!" he appealed to the other passengers.

"Come and take this damned old lunatic off my hands!" I shouted, still holding on to him.

And so as we surged back and forth and other passengers began climbing over seats to get to us, a gong sounded and a moment later the car ran down on the siding at Aegia and the doors flew open.

CHAPTER 12

We must have been fifteen hundred feet above the earth and from that high altitude had a most magnificent view. Mountains could be seen in the blue distance, and rivers winding through sunny fields with here and there a lake that flashed like silver. Many towns and villages were visible from where we floated high up in midair, trains of cars far below us looked like great, black, jointed worms crawling swiftly along the earth and the crispness of the rarefied atmosphere would have chilled us but for the exercise of driving the great double aeroplane.

It was exhilarating to the highest degree as we swung around in great ascending circles or hurtled quivering down through the air in long toboggan slides, to leap up again as though sprung from a catapult, when the steering fan was dipped. Helen Morris never looked more beautiful than as we swung side by side under the aeroplane and surveyed the panorama of the earth below. During the year of our acquaintance, I had made no more progress in loving or love making than on the first day we met. Always kind, sympathetic, sometimes almost tender, she nevertheless held me at a worshipful distance, never repulsing, but always repressing me in a way that convinced me that my suit was not disagreeable—but hopeless. No slighting reference had been made to Professor Hallam since the day when in her impetuous argument with her father she sneered at the fiddlers of Ironia, and indeed, her conduct afterward indicated repentance for her hasty and unjust words, for in her subsequent manner toward him in my presence she seemed desirous to make atonement by being especially kind. She was interested in me, that I was sure of, and when I achieved some notoriety by winning the somewhat famous "gangplow" case against the state, and began to be talked about as the brilliant attorney from America, her elation was so sincere and apparent as to give me the hope that I had won two suits at the same time; but when I would have improved the occasion to press my claim for her heart and hand, she protested declaring with tears that I gave her great pain and begged me to desist. Notwithstanding, she seemed to be happier with me than with Professor Hallam and I reached the conclusion after close observation that her hand had been promised to him and she was too proud or too true to draw back when she found that her heart could not be given with it. I had yielded to my fate and while improving every opportunity to bask in her presence. I no more spoke of my love. But this glorious afternoon I found it hard to repress the promptings of my heart. She looked so happy and all nature seemed so glad, that I could not bring myself to feel that I was a finally rejected lover.

The novelty and delight of my position made me again to doubt the reality of it all and looking into her eyes that beamed as tender as the blue sky above us. I said, "this must be heaven materialized and modernized."

"If so, then a good many features were eliminated in the process," replied my fair companion.

"I care not what is lacking so long as that feature which makes it heaven be here." I said, looking straight into her deep brown eyes.

"And pray what is that?" she asked.

"The angelic!"

"But for the testimony of the Good Book which records that

he was cast out. I would be tempted to retort that Lucifer is also in evidence," she replied blushing and laughing.

"His was a sad fate," said I, "but not so sad as mine, for he was shut out forever from the sight of the bliss which he had lost, while I, alas, must endure the double grief of losing what is more than heaven to me and then seeing another enjoy what I have lost!" She blushed deeply and dropped her eyes before my ardent gaze, and then turning her head looked away toward the blue hills that broke the northern horizon.

"After all," she said, and speaking as much to herself as to me, "after all, the Christian philosophy teaches that the real heaven and true, the peace which is above all earthly passion, is as much the fruit of sacrifice as of love." And turning her eyes full upon me, "perverse and impulsive as I am sometimes, I yet believe that I am capable of suffering rather than that I should be the willful cause of suffering in another."

I began vehemently to protest against any philosophy that would make two people miserable for the chance of making one happy, when my ear caught the sound of a wavering melody above us, which seemed to come down from heaven itself.

"Hark! What is that sweet sound?"

My companion listened a moment and then her face clouded. "Don't you know? That is Professor Hallam and his Aeolian harp following us. Let's dip!" and jerking the steering fan with all her force, we flew down an aerial incline five hundred feet or more with such velocity as almost to take my breath. In making these dips or downward glides, only a slight inclination is necessary to send the aeroplane whizzing through the air with the speed of an arrow, but my companion, either with reckless abandon or by accident, threw our machine down almost to an angle of forty-five degrees and when, at the bottom of the incline, the head was thrown up to make it leap into the air again, the great aeroplane bellied upward with a strain that made the frame bend and quiver and then with a report like the

ch. ends p. 145

crack of a pistol it burst almost from end to end and seeming to shudder for a moment, began to drop toward the earth.

In this moment of deadly peril, I believe that all that was best and noblest in me asserted itself and like a flash it occurred to me that the rent[1] canvas, while not sufficient to bear up two, would probably drop gently enough with one to avoid fatal consequences. With the thought came the resolve and in less than a second after the aeroplane began to fall I had thrown loose the strap that bound me to my seat and rising upon the pedal leaned over until my lips almost touched the blanched face of the woman I loved and shouted (for the whipping of the rent canvas made a noise like that of a hurricane), "it is death for one and I love you and can die for you!"

"Then let it be death for both," she cried letting go of the bar and throwing both arms around my neck with a vice-like grip, "for I love you and cannot live without you!"

"One kiss, oh my darling!" pressing my lips to hers with a thrill that made me to forget the peril of death, and then throwing myself forward, dropped from the pedal. But the fair arms about my neck were strong and though I struggled to break loose, knowing that the velocity at which we were falling meant certain death for both of us, they held me fast. Down, down we fell with a quivering fluttering motion like a winged bird dropping to earth, and choked to blindness and suffocation I was expecting to feel the impact that would crush us against the ground, when I became dimly conscious of a fierce shrieking sound above us and then our downward motion seemed to be arrested. A moment later, we struck the earth with a shock that seemed to break every bone in my body. With a great wave of thankfulness I realized that we were saved and, disengaging the fair arms that still wound around my neck like bands of steel, I struggled to my feet and, hastily unbuckling the strap

---

[1] Torn.

that bound the beautiful form of my heart's idol to the wrecked machine, dragged her fainting from under the aeroplane.

My first concern was to ascertain if she were killed or injured and, laying her gently on the grass, I found to my unspeakable joy that she was alive and bore no marks of injury. Loosing the close fitting bodice at the throat that she might breathe more freely, and fanning her vigorously with my handkerchief, I was rewarded in a few moments by seeing her open her eyes and look up at me with an expression of inexpressible tenderness.

"Oh, my love!" she said holding up her hands to me, "then you would indeed have died for me!"

"A thousand times," I cried rapturously, seizing her hands and covering them with kisses. "Now you shall be mine forever and ever!"

"No, no, it cannot be!" she exclaimed hastily, withdrawing her hands and springing to her feet. "What does this mean?" running back to the aeroplane with an expression of terror. I followed her and saw with astonishment that another aeroplane was foul with ours and lay upon it.

"What indeed!" I cried, seizing the end of it and lifting it up.

"Oh, don't you—can't you see that it is Professor Hallam's? Don't you see his harp? Oh my God!" and with a shuddering cry of horror she covered her face with her hands and fell upon her knees moaning and crying.

Then it dawned upon me that the noble man had swooped down and attaching his machine to ours had thrown himself to death to save our lives! Leaving the weeping woman I ran to a group of people who had gathered some little distance away and were talking and gesticulating wildly and there, crushed and dead, lay the noblest man and greatest genius that ever lived. In his Godlike nobility of soul, he had caught our aeroplane several hundred feet above the earth and seeing that it could not sustain all and prevent us from being crushed against the earth, he had thrown himself down to a horrible death that

ch. ends next p.

his affianced[2] might escape with his rival! I wonder not that at last, when earthly passion had been chilled by the cold touch of death and the dross of mortality scarce intervened, that it was of him she thought, that it was the wondrous melody of his nocturne that she heard above the roaring of the frozen sea, rolling down from the beyond ere[3] she passed. And I felt no pang of jealousy! If, in the house of many mansions, (where there is no marrying and giving in marriage, but all are as the angels of God in love and purity)—I may be accounted worthy of the humblest station in their sphere, I shall be content. And yet she loved me and not him!

Kneeling by him I raised the noble head and chafed the poor broken hands that held within them the potency of such divine harmony as the world will never hear again, but the great soul had passed! Death was doubtless instantaneous, for though his face was unmarred his body was horribly crushed and broken. Dispatching one of the bystanders to convey intelligence of the accident to the city. I went back and raised the weeping girl who was to have been the dead man's wife.

"My darling," I said lifting her gently, "you would have been true to him and he was a Godlike man and worthy of your troth,[4] but surely the hand of providence is in this terrible thing. Will you go and look upon him?"

Taking my arm without speaking I led her to where our savior lay upon the ground and with a solemn grace and dignity that was really majestic, she walked around to the dead man's feet and looked long and calmly at his face.

"Thou wert too pure and great to be loved as a man," she spoke at last, "and in the presence of thy dead clay I feel as unworthy as Guinevere[5] at the feet of the pure and royal

---

[2] Bound in a pledge of marriage; betrothed.
[3] Before.
[4] Faith or loyalty.
[5] In Arthurian legend, Queen Guinevere was the wife of King Arthur, and mistress of the knight Lancelot, one of the greatest Knights of the Round Table.

Arthur. Alas! the world has lost its greatest spirit and I a friend of whom I could never be worthy!" Then, as I led her away, "Oh my Lancelot, thou art not and never can be so good or great a man, and yet I love you!"

CHAPTER 13

For months, my beautiful wife had been fading like a flower. Even on shipboard and amid the excitement of the wildest storm, she seemed listless and totally indifferent to her surroundings.

The boding sadness that began to come upon her after the terrible accident that resulted in the death of Professor Hallam never left her, and while she sometimes simulated vivacity, her gaiety pained rather than pleased me, for my love penetrated her sweet little deception and I knew that it was for my sake that she pretended what she did not feel.

I had fondly hoped, and so had her parents, that when she was out of the country, and away from the scenes that reminded her of her past, her old buoyancy of spirits would return. Indeed but for this and the dreadful melancholia that grew upon her day after day, we would never have yielded to her desire to undertake the desperate journey to America. But it was not so, and the bitterness of my disappointment amounted to anguish. Every morning on board of the vessel, as on shore, she would awake at the exact moment when the wonderful matins of Professor Hallam had been wont to roll out from the tower of music, and listen wide-eyed and with every faculty strained to the utmost tension of alertness, listening. And as I lay beside her sometimes and held her hand, feigning sleep, I could feel the nervous tremor that agitated her, while her pulse fluttered with the intensity of the nervous strain.

My God! It was terrible that my sweet wife, the most beautiful and gracious woman I ever knew and the only one I ever loved should suffer like that! And at sunset she would listen for the nocturne with the same fever of excitement. Thus as long as we were in latitudes where day and night alternated and when we reached the regions of the pole where there were no sun risings nor settings, instead of becoming better she grew worse, and this intense, preoccupied, listening attitude became habitual. I employed every artifice I could devise to interest her and fix her attention on objects about us and she with the sweetest grace tried to be interested, but even as I held her hand and talked to her with all the animation I could affect, looking into the fathomless depths of her glorious eyes I would lose her. With the most intense concentration of mind she would follow me and "sense" what I was saying for a few minutes, and then she listened indeed, but not to me! And oh, she tried so hard!

One evening we stood by the rail on the quarterdeck looking out over the hissing brine at the sun, which hung red upon the horizon. It seemed as if it were just ready to sink out of sight though really it had been but slightly above the horizon for many days. As I stood with one arm around her and holding her hand, her gaze was fixed on the red ball of fire that touched the ocean's rim and which was reflected in her eyes like the flashes in an opal. I drew her to me and spoke ardently of what I hoped to accomplish when we reached my own country, even putting my face against hers as I spoke. But I do not think she heard me! Like one hypnotized she seemed totally oblivious of her surroundings, and I saw with a pang of anguish that she was listening for the strains of that glorious nocturne, such as was never heard except from the "tower of music," and such as was never played by any hand save that of the dead master.

And then I believed my heart broke! Then a pain struck through my breast that has never ceased from that hour to this, waking or sleeping.

Dropping her hand I fell forward with a groan and catching the rail rested my head upon it. Starting as if she had been struck, my darling came back to herself, and with a cry fell down at my feet and with a torrent of broken words and sobs begged me to forgive her.

"Oh my love!" she cried, as the tears ran down her beautiful upturned face, "my heart is breaking for you, but I cannot help it, indeed I cannot. Oh! when I cannot see you or hear you my heart aches for you with never ceasing misery. I have struggled and I have prayed, but God will not help me! And I have feared that you—that you might not understand—that you might think—Oh what shall I say? That you might not think that I love you and you only with all my heart! Oh my husband pity me and forgive your poor miserable, unfortunate wife! Oh I—Oh, oh—" and she fell forward with her face against my knees, sobbing and quivering with the violence of her emotion.

Lifting her gently in my arms while my heart was bursting, I carried her down into the cabin and laid her on her bed and with her arms still about my neck as when they held me back from a fearful death that summer afternoon. I fell on my knees by the bedside and with my face against hers, wept with her. And in the dim twilight of the cabin, while the sun hung red upon the rim of the sea, and the billows rustled along the vessel's side with a sad murmur like the sighing of an autumn wind, she told me that Professor Hallam's music had always impressed her in a way she could not understand. That whenever she heard his wonderful matins and nocturnes she seemed to lose herself, and was borne away on the billows of harmonious sound.

She told me that she could even divine the music in advance of the playing and knew each bar before she heard it as well as if she had composed it herself. Stranger than all, she said she always knew by some mysterious influence the very moment

ch. ends p. 155

the music was going to begin, and she knew by that influence, that mysterious something, that the master was playing now, was playing all the time, and while she could not hear the music, by this strange power which dominated her, she felt it and knew what unutterable strains were being rendered in heaven or somewhere. She told me as she lay there with her soft arms about my neck and her dear face touching mine, that if she had the skill to set it down fast enough she could write the grand music that was being rendered day and night and day after day without cessation! At first, she said she only felt it evenings and mornings, and then more and more, until finally when we passed into the zone where there was no alternation of day and night, she felt that he was playing all the time! She could not hear it but she felt it, felt its beauty and could not escape its power! She had kept this from me till now, seeing my suffering, she could no longer conceal it, but told me all, that I might not doubt her love, but pity and forgive her the pain she caused me!

If she had done this at first, the great physicians of Ironia might have cured her of the malady—for such it must have been—and I entreated her to let me take her back then, but she would not consent. "Why it has stopped now!" she cried, holding my face between her hands and looking up at me with the love light in her eyes. "It stopped short off when you fell against the rail, and I know he would never play again even to the angels if he knew it caused me sorrow!"

And as I gazed into her face and saw the old look in her eyes I thanked God and prayed that the spell might be broken, and that she might never again fall under the power of the dead man's music.

I knew not that the end was so near and when it came, it was as if God had struck me with a thunderbolt out of a clear sky. For a week, she had not come on deck and had scarcely been on her feet during the time. The hallucination that possessed her had not recurred since the day she told me all and I was sure that in some inexplicable way her violent emotion at that time had been the means of breaking the spell. But the improvement I had looked for from that did not come and she grew weaker, physically, day by day—or rather from hour to hour, as there was no alternation of day and night.

We had sighted "Barrington Strait" and was laying off and on, keeping the towering ice wall in sight and waiting for a wind that would drive us through the current that runs like a millrace through the channel. For hours my beautiful wife, now so frail and white as to seem almost ethereal, had reclined on the lounge in the cabin with her eyes half closed and such an expression of heavenly peace upon her face that I felt awed as though in the presence of an angel. I was sitting at a table trying to fix my mind upon a chart that I was making of the ice coast and the entrance to the strait, when with a slight cry she clasped her hands and opened wide her eyes with that look of listening expectancy I knew so well.

Springing to her side with a half uttered imprecation, I kneeled beside her and caught her clasped hands in mine. "Listen," she whispered excitedly, "he is going to play! I feel it—ah, now he is playing! It is the glorious nocturne he played that evening when we were by the river. Hark! I can hear it—oh, so grand!"

ch. ends p. 155

Her eyes closed and she moved her head forward and front side to side for some moments keeping time.

"Edward, my husband, where are you?"

"I am here, darling." I cried passionately, pressing her hands and imprinting a kiss on her partly opened lips.

"Then I am content," and withdrawing one of her hands from mine, she put an arm around my neck. I started to speak caressingly to her when she stopped me with a quick, "hush, I am to sing. He is playing the prelude! Now he is motioning me to begin, now!" and inhaling a deep breath she began to sing the great "Peace Hymn" of the Republic:

> "Of old when down the stargirt[1] sky,
> The angel voices swelled and ran,
> This was the burden of their cry,
> Peace, peace on earth, good will to man."

In the refrain,

> "Peace, peace, peace, on all the earth peace.
> Peace, peace, peace, among all men peace."

Her voice swelled grandly and floated out over the black ocean. She drew my face down upon her bosom and as the triumphant notes of this magnificent hymn—the masterpiece of Professor Hallam—rose and fell, my heart seemed to melt within me, my tears gushed forth and I felt as if my spirit was out borne on the wings of song, far above the sphere of earthly hope and passion; beyond the sound of discord, beyond the veil of darkness, into a great luminous ethereal space that throbbed with the rhythmic measures of the music of the spheres. And as I floated upward on the waves of unutterable melody where there was no horizon and no sky, an angel held me by the hand and about the neck and that angel, I felt, had been my wife!

---

[1] Surrounded by stars.

I was aroused by a touch on the shoulder, and looking up I saw the kind face of Captain Brent bending over me. "Where am I?" I asked in a dazed way.

"You are in the hands of Almighty God," replied the Captain solemnly, "who doeth all things well."

I staggered to my feet and gazed about me and then looking down saw the earthly image of my wife still and white as a reclining statue of marble; her eyes were closed as though in slumber, and her lips were parted with a smile, and I realized that God had struck me the final blow. With a calmness, I could not understand. I motioned him out of the cabin and bowed myself in the presence of my dead.

When I went on deck again the sun had disappeared below the horizon and fingers of golden fire pointed from the rim of the black ocean to the zenith that was flushed with rosy light.

But why should I linger with these sorrowful details? I was not stirred by any emotion and felt nothing except that dull pain in my heart, which has never left me. Captain Brent was like a father and the boys pressed my hand with a silent sympathy that expressed far more than words.

I say I was not moved by any great emotion, except once, when, after Captain Brent had read the solemn service for those who are buried in the sea and motioned to the mate to take me into his cabin while they committed my idol to the deep, then for a time I was crazed. I had nearly gone mad and I believe I would have killed every man aboard the ship before I would have suffered them to cast that loved form into the cold hissing waters of that black sea.

ch. ends next p.

The weather was favorable and as the billows rolled over and far up on the shelving ledge of the great berg, we had only to ride in on the crest of a wave and drawing the boat up make it fast on the ice.

It was a little mountain of ice and snow and tapering up from the water line it terminated in two glittering pinnacles like crystal spires of a cathedral of glass. Between the two a niche or grotto partly filled with snow and up to this, we climbed by throwing ropes over the jutting crags and lesser pinnacles that projected from the sloping sides above the wash of the sea waves. And so we toiled up from terrace to terrace and from pinnacle to pinnacle until we reached the grot[2] between the spires and there we placed the couch with the earthly form of my beautiful wife and banked the snow about it. Below the black sea sobbed and moaned about the base of the great iceberg, and above the wind sang among the crevices and pinnacles of the resonant ice like a hundred Aeolian harps, swelling in fitful gusts until the triumphant chords rang out like strains from the "tower of music," and there we left her a marble queen upon a crystal throne, alone with God and the angels.

I begged for the love of heaven to be left there with her, but cruel in their kindness they dragged me away to the ship.

And then there burst upon us a scene of unearthly splendor. The aurora australis sprang up around us, and under it, the black sea turned to gold, frosted here and there with the foaming crests of billows.

Every rope and spar of the ship stood out white in the

[2] Grotto.

spectral light and the great icebergs in their whiteness and still-
ness and silence, looked like ghosts preternaturally enlarged.

The twin spires of the crystal mausoleum gleamed like sap-
phires and in the grot between, magnified by the wondrous
light and irradiated by its ineffable glory was revealed the form
of my lost wife. And while the amber and golden light played
around the towering berg, radiating from it like a halo, fluttering
like banners and angels wings above it, we drew away until it
became a mere flashing gem upon the sea of gold.

Richard Jameson Morgan
HONORARY HEATHEN

THE STATE WAS
MADE FOR MAN,
AND NOT MAN
FOR THE STATE.